The Grand Royal Stand-off and Other Stories

Thomas F. Sheehan

Pocol Press

Punxsutawney, PA

POCOL PRESS
Published in the United States of America
by Pocol Press
320 Sutton Street
Punxsutawney, PA 15767
www.pocolpress.com

© 2019 by Thomas F. Sheehan

All rights reserved. No part of this book may be reproduced in any form whatsoever without the express written consent of Pocol Press. Exceptions are made for brief quotations for criticism and reviews.

Publisher's Cataloguing-in-Publication

Names: Sheehan, Thomas F., 1928-
Title: The Grand Royal stand-off and other stories / Thomas F. Sheehan.
Description: Punxsutawney, PA: Pocol Press, 2019.
Identifiers: LCCN 2019945243 | ISBN 978-1-929763-89-4
Subjects: LCSH Frontier and pioneer life--West (U.S.)--Fiction. | Cowboys--Fiction. | Indians of North America--Fiction. | West (U.S.)--Fiction. | Short stories, American. | Western stories. | Historical fiction. | BISAC FICTION / Westerns | FICTION / Short Stories (single author).
Classification: LCC PS3569.H39216 G73 2019 | DDC 813.6--dc23

Library of Congress Control Number: 2019945243

ACKNOWLEDGEMENTS

Stories in this collection, over a stretch of time, have appeared in various sites or presentations- on-line such as *Facebook*, *Rope and Wire Western-Style Magazine*, *Frontier Tales*, *Literally Stories*, *Merida Review*, *Danse Macabre*, and *Cowboy Jamboree*. Some stories were presented in sites or magazines that are now defunct. All rights belong to me, Tom Sheehan, as author and agreement.

TABLE OF CONTENTS

The Grand Royal Stand-off at Darby's Creek	1
The Marshal's Widow	6
Stud Carbon, Free from Jail, Bound to Search	10
The Carney Boys	13
The Kid on Three Legs	17
Chaz Brandin, Gunman Extraordinaire	20
Jess Hardy's Studies of Wolf Packs	23
Knot Bretwell, New Deputy	25
The Drifter	29
Brett Kirkness and the Bandits	33
The Conquistadors in New Pants	36
Al La Cazenza and the Letter to the Lady on a Golden Palomino	41
Joshua Jenks, Odds to Evens	45
Sherman "Shakie" Tucker and Golden Mary	48
The Passage of Apollo Greysmith	53
Tracy Kurt Elbert, Bumbler by Birth	62
Joey Charlo and the Big Black Bear	65
The Small War of Kurt Knobson	68
Being a Cowtown Santa for a Time	72
Ransom Doak, Shooter Extraordinaire	79
A Freighter's Connection	82
Micah Topaz, Born Sheriff	87
Teddie Silverado's My Name	90
The Wagon Master Finds a Lady	94
Call Me Chef	99
Greg Knighthawk, Sheriff, Taxico County	106
Pete Rowes and the Way It Goes	109
The Cowtown Candlemaker	113
The Old Man from Dry Harbor	116
Turf Malloy's Squeaky Dreams	119

The Grand Royal Stand-off at Darby's Creek

Willard Joseph Lord Puffington, late colonel of the 1st Regiment of Hodson's Horse, India-released, Asia-departed, separated from the British Army in 1870, reined in his horse at the head of Darby's Creek as it flowed from the heart of earth in the Rockies foothills. His trained eye had found a minor change in the geography from the previous day; the small tree at the crest of one hummock had moved ("Been moved," he muttered) to another hummock closer to the wagon train's position. The year was 1873; he was working for a wagon master as the wagon train was set to renew its journey on another day, its destination a valley in far California, his new education in progress.

Puffington, astride a black stallion he had coveted from first site, a 16-hander with fire in his eyes, summoned the wagon master, Bruce Wilcox, to his place at the head of the lead wagon about to move off on a new day.

Puffington, to a casual observer, could have been a Royal Archer, a Knight at the Round Table, or Her Majesty's Consort, he sat so noble a position on the huge stallion, as if he were in command even though he was not in command, not on this wagon train, not yet. A highly rugged and handsome man of deep-well blue eyes that never seemed to rest for long on one spot, he possessed a stern chin signifying his make-up, and premature gray hair looking as if it had never been trimmed,

"See anything out there, Bruce," he said to Wilcox, "that is subtlely different from yesterday evening when we rolled up?" He pointed off in the general direction of the foothills and timberlines to the north.

Wilcox, himself a most rugged individual, nearly as handsome as Puffington in a distinctive western outfit, scanned the area with his experienced eye developed on six other trains he had led west. "At the outset I'd have to say the only thing that could be different is that single tree on the small rise. Nothing out there seems possible to be different, but I can't mark it as different, Will. Can you?"

"Yes," Puffington said. "Yesterday, or last evening, from this exact spot, I had it marked in line with that rocky peak that's off to the left of it now. I stood exactly here, at the head of this wagon and marked it with that peak ... three objects in a row ... my position, the tree, and the far peak. What we called a syzygy in my astronomy courses."

"A what? A syzygy? What the hell is a syzygy, if that's how you say it, Will?" He shook his head in wonder and realized that Puffington had certainly been exposed to more educated matters than he himself had.

"Well, Bruce, picture this ... the sun's out there, the moon passes between it and us here on Earth and an eclipse occurs. That's three spatial bodies in a row when the eclipse happens. Syzygy is what I first thought was a made-up word with the three Zs in it, to account for the three heavenly bodies, but it really comes from the Greek."

"Oh," Bruce said, "like it's all Greek to me."

"Anyway," Puffington added, moved by the humor, "what that means is we are being scouted upon."

Wilcox said, "Let's rush out there from two directions and nab whoever, see what's up."

Puffington, nodding, moved back into his military experience, calling up similar situations, or seeking similar ones. That recall went back 15 years, to 1858 and a campaign against the Naserabad Brigade of rebels led by the Rajah of Gonder. The rebels used numerous single scouts, or spies, posted alone in open areas of the plains, under the meanest and simplest of cover, to report on positions and strengths of the British Colonial forces. They were to be so obviously posted that they might not be seen; in the plans of things, to be overlooked by less tested men.

In that Colonial command he too had a number of volunteer-type men of extraordinary courage and guile, and rather than send a force out to rout the spies, he sent a few of these volunteers out to obvious positions to take, kill, or rout the spies located there. To a man they were successful, and two rebels were captured and one was killed in a running fight. The night went silent after the last hand-to-hand encounter. Puffington could not envision how many soldiers' lives had been saved by the actions of a few men for good of all the force. Subsequently he had introduced commendations into the personnel records of the three men.

Now their heroics, and the inestimable results, came back full force into his planning.

Having made up his mind, the former British colonel, marker of men, measurer of talents, saw one man of the wagon train emerge as his choice for a select operation.

He asked Wilcox, "Can you spare Max Malvern for a short foray into enemy territory? It should not take too long, but that's only a guess from my experience long ago in a similar situation."

"He's as good as any man you can pick, Will," Wilcox affirmed. "Sly as a fox he is, quick as a night coyote, quiet as a spider on a single strand. He won't say so but he'd be honored to be selected."

He waved to a small and wiry man sitting on a big gray across the circle of wagons, and the man dismounted, tied off his horse and walked slowly toward them as if he were carrying a large burden. His face was covered with a dark beard sitting under a black hat as wide as his shoulders, with a ribbon on it lined with fish hooks caught up in the fabric.

In the rifle scabbard on his horse could be seen two bamboo poles along with his long-barreled Sharps rifle. In one glance Max Malvern appeared as a survivor of both the plains and the mountain life, with a turn at water in the mix.

Malvern approached, nodded at both men and stood as quiet as a stump.

"Max," Bruce Wilcox said, "the colonel has a small task he'd like you to do. He'll explain it."

Puffington pointed off at the singular small tree on the hummock. "See that slight tree on that mound out there, Max, how it seems to sit all by itself?"

Malvern looked and said, "You mean it ain't most likely alone even as we look at it and you want to make sure of that one way or t'other?"

"Exactly, Max," Puffington said, smiling widely, "and without them knowing they are being approached if at all possible."

"Be glad to take a peek, Colonel. Been by there yestidy and know the ground. Take care of it rightly." He turned around and walked back to his horse and rode to the far side of the circled wagons nearing departure. Much as a prairie phantom he disappeared into a dip in the grass.

A few hours later, the wagon train on its way finally, the circle of wagons nearly in a long line on the grassy trail, Malvern slipped up behind a man, a white man, dressed clumsily as a redskin. The knife was at the man's throat when he woke up from a sound clubbing on the head. He was tied across the rump of Malvern's horse.

The wily scout tickled in a decidedly devilish manner the throat of the fake Indian, drawing the keen blade in a slow sweep across the man's neck.

Malvern said, "I tell you, son, you got some hurtin' comin' your way from the Colonel who's almost right outta Inja where they was inventin' punishment afore we was even here. Heard him talkin' one night back at the big river about how they put a leaky water tin near a man in irons and don't give him a sip for more days that the trouble's worth. The colonel, once't we get back to the wagons, is some set in his ways. He's got some steep talkin' to do and you got yourself some steep thinkin' on how you're gonna keep breathin'. These things ain't really gonna sit like puddin' with him 'cause he's all soljer."

The return to the wagon was completed without incident for Malvern and his prisoner.

Puffington was quite pleased at the sight of Malvern riding in with a prisoner, the prisoner slumped over and obviously beaten into submission. He was impressed with Malvern's foray amongst the enemy, or at their fringes.

"You've done a unique job, Max. My compliments to you. I assume there was not much resistance offered."

"Oh," replied Malvern, "he didn't waste none of my time. And we didn't waste no time comin' back here, as I figure he's got a pile of stuff to unload on you. I brung his own horse too."

The prisoner talked. "My name's Oliver Gordsen. They broke me out of jail back in Ashburn more'n a year ago. Just took me into the gang long as I did what they wanted. I was just a drunk caught in the mix, and them, those fellers, are all murderers. They don't care who they kill. I swear to God I ain't kilt any man yet."

"Be easy, son," Puffington said. "How many are there, what armaments do they have, who's the leader, and is he a military man?" He patted Gordsen on the back.

"How'd you know all that?" the prisoner said. "We got about 35-40 men, one Gattling gun stole from the army back before Trumont Fort was finished being built, and the boss, Luther Buckston, used to be a colonel in the Confederate Army and still hates anything blue. He swears to God the South is coming back someday."

"What are they planning, Oliver?" Puffington said, his voice light and casual and somewhat friendly, his hand sitting lightly on Gordsen's shoulder. "You must consider luckily that you are no longer a part of that organization, you're no longer one of those murderers. Your part in the coming hostilities is, by my estimation, now ceased." He paused, and then said, "But you can be somewhat accountable if certain things are not accomplished beforehand."

It was as veiled a threat as ever uttered.

Gordsen, uneasy in a sudden turn, said, "What do I gotta do?"

"Tell us where and when they propose to attack us. With what size force at first. The placement of the Gattling gun at the chosen site. The second effort of the attack. And a third, if there is one."

Puffington tapped him lightly again on the shoulder. "It's as easy as eating porridge pie, Oliver. Just as easy."

Gordsen, as if he were reading from a battle plan, laid everything out for them; it was crystal clear to both Puffington and Wilcox.

"They'd have us in the cross hairs," Wilcox chirped, "but can we trust what he's telling us?"

"Oh, it had better be the truth, Bruce. We better come out ahead in this. I am leaving all these details on paper so that if we do lose, that one-time Confederate colonel will know who set him up, one way or the other."

He turned to Gordsen and said, "Of course, Oliver, you understand my position, don't you?"

Gordsen, a minor man to begin with, but with a sudden weight taken off him by his delivery of information, said, "I do. I do. They are plain all-out murderers. I'm glad I'm on your side."

Puffington looked him in the eye and said, "It's not just that easy, Oliver. I'm going to let you go tonight. We are going to have a sudden halt with some obvious mechanical problems with two of our wagons. We will re-circle them this evening just this side of the entrance to the gorge where they plan to hit us. We are going to wait there for two days for federal troops to arrive in two days. They will clear the way for us through the gorge. There will be no killing of the lead animals and the rear animals hauling the wagons to lock us completely within the gorge, subject at length to careful and methodical killing, stealing, raping and ravaging the people of this wagon train."

The suave retired Colonial colonel patted Gordsen again on the shoulder, like a father to whom an adolescent son had admitted a minor mischief. "I know you can carry it off, Oliver. I have utmost faith in you."

"You got my word, Colonel."

Before Gordsen was let go that night in darkness, well after two wagons had called a halt with obvious mechanical problems having developed, he was allowed to hear Puffington say, as carefully planned as could be arranged without alerting the prisoner of the ruse, that the troops were really due that very night, a full force of a command that would hit the gorge with all their might, and it would be of no avail to let the enemy know that fact.

"The vise is in place," Puffington was heard to say by Gordsen, who was being let go on his own horse, with his own guns, but with no ammunition, no water in his canteen, no way to go but ahead to the gorge and the brigand force, the way slyly shown to him by Max Malvern who had captured him in the first place.

In a few hours, at the ready for an hour or more, under dark skies and a wind whipping out of the southwest, the wagon train fled through the gorge led by the retired colonel of the 1st Regiment of Hodson's Horse, a most gallant troop of Colonial Cavalry, as fast as gloried Cossacks, as quick as the swift Gurkhas in a downhill attack, and as steadfast as drovers of the new west bringing the herd home.

The Marshal's Widow

Deloris *Di Di* Walters was alone and just about starting her second year as a lonely widow when she saw the rider coming her way, over the small rise at his back, along with a sky of far blue. The way he sat in the saddle told her he was a stranger and not anyone she had ever seen in Porto Blanco, her hometown south a way, or here in Pegasus, where Deke Walters brought her to live. It all seemed so long ago, she could scarcely fill in any time or events with a clear background. Much of it, except the happiest moments she had spent with the man she loved, had faded in a hurry.

And she had rarely spent a moment alone with any man, friend, acquaintance or casual visitor for a whole year, left alone by those who knew her best.

And she did not know the man coming her way. He rode with his sombrero tipped back on his head, as if to show off his features. He was young, handsome, light of face, pinkish from the sun, perhaps a blond who knew his way around women. That thought lingered in her mind, touched a few strings in her body. He let them be.

Something told her times had changed, life had changed. She hoped her face wouldn't change so readily, as it had in the past. Deke had said, "I call it *announcement*," in a way that also told her it was special, "Best be on your toes, on guard, but things will change, they always change."

She felt no guilt, no shame, no sense of remorse.

The young rider hailed her from a social distance, also an announcement of sorts: "Hello, the house, a horse and rider have need of water. Can we rest by your well? We won't tarry long." He added, in quick introduction, "My name is Jack Burton and I used to work for the KTL Ranch back east of us and we called it The Kettle and there were often 50 of us at a time tending cattle and horses. But I don't work there anymore. Just out here on my own now, drifting around."

The short tarry was still active a few hours later, after water share, after lunch invitation on her own dare, finding him charming, soft spoken, polite, doing all kinds of menial tasks about the kitchen after the meal, not unlike Deke. Dishes were out of the way, the table cleared.

Di Di fixed her hair in a small mirror, wished she had braided it earlier that morning.

Things changed in another quick announcement as they sat at the table. "Ma'am," Jack Burton said, "I did not come here accidentally or without purpose, and, as I say on my honor, a dying man posted me to provide information to you on the death of your husband. Your husband, Marshal Deke Walters, was shot in the back as part of a dual assassination attempt, the other half incomplete. That other name has to be held in secret for the time being. I was charged with this mission by the dying man who issued the order of death be brought down on your husband in his employ by another man, if you can follow the line."

His obvious pause led him to admit, "The dying man was my father who carried a worried soul about near his whole life."

Burton, for a deep minute, seemed to allow himself some recovery of his aims in the matter. "I'm left with the bad part which might turn out to be good for you, because somewhere, along the line, someone said there's gold on this property of yours."

Di Di Walters found quick misery come back over her with the announced change, knowing that life indeed had changed and her comfort outlook hit by the abrupt turn of events. She cringed, found a tear or two on her cheek, cried a bit and begged for more information, saying with open honesty, "He was an honest man, my husband. He wore his badge with pride and with confidence."

Regathered, she added, "I also knew Deke had an enemy or two. All law officers do, just about every one of them, as he allowed, but you make it an organized effort that says it's more than one man. Why does that surprise me?"

"It's the plain awful truth, Ma'am. The plain awful truth, like he was plain in the way of someone else's gain. I know my pa near carried it to his death, until I came along on a mere whim, like I had nothing else in the world to do but save a man's soul at his death bed."

The more Jack Burton spoke, the more he admitted with each statement, or each announcement, the more she felt a growing sense of comfort and the growing glow that had begun inside her. It was a warmth she had forgotten, the way it filled her chest, made strange sounds in her throat that she hoped were not loud enough for him to hear, sent quick little messages to her brain, telling her she was being captured again by a man of character. Love and glory often made suitable starts that made entry easy on one's own soul.

For a moment she thought of kissing him immediately to cut short all the feelings that they'd have to expend if love was coming upon them, and all because death itself had different hands in the quick arrival, real death of real people, people they had loved with all the right intentions and right purposes and felt shared back to them.

"So," she said, "if you can't tell me who else is involved here, it must be someone I know here in Pegasus, or even in Porto Blanco, my hometown. That has to be the way it is; someone I know or trust or have dealt with. That gets pretty scary, don't you think? Knife at my throat in the hand of someone's husband, or a friend of Deke's, or the saloon owner and barkeep, Dutch Hartford, or even the new sheriff whose name I can't remember right now. That means I shouldn't even go into town alone, nor let anybody close enough to this cabin like I let you."

"I'm real glad you see it that way, Ma'am, and it's all true and if you go you have to go there with me and my pistols," and he quick-drew them each in the instant and the light caught like flashes on both weapons, and she hadn't yet blinked her eyes at the fast-draw, the quickest she had ever seen.

Another sweep of sudden trust and confidence surged through her body. "That's awful fast," she uttered, and added, "Did I name him yet without giving up his name?"

"Close as cow smell, Di Di." It was the first time he had used her name, and it came mellow and comforting to her ears, and in that special place in her heart.

That's when Di Di Walters kissed a man for the first time since her husband had died. It gathered all things good into her.

Jack Burton suggested a maneuver of sorts. "Why don't we go into town this evening and get this all over with. It's hung on you too long and we might clear the whole thing up in one big hurry."

Di Di accepted the suggestion and kissed him again.

They were like a pair of strangers riding into Pegasus down the dusty main road before the sun had set, yet all eyes on them, and one man rushed to get to the saloon, calling out as he entered, "Hey, Dutch, Di Di Walters is comin' into town with that new guy we was all talkin' 'bout last night, the kid with the shiny pistols."

Dutch, as we might suspect, knew everything that was said or went on in the saloon, in Pegasus, and most of the territory, for that matter. And knew just where the gold was on Di Di's place, courtesy of an habitual drunk assigned by him to keep his eye on Di Di. When he told Dutch what he saw, Dutch got him drunk enough to walk out back of the saloon and get belted on the head, to be found dead in the morning.

He took a rifle off the wall and laid it across the bar top, facing directly at the entrance. It looked ominous and deadly and several tables in the line of fire were quickly abandoned.

But nobody left the saloon.

When Di Di and Jack Burton walked in, they were in the line of fire.

Panic raced through Dutch Hartford, including down one arm and the hand reaching for the trigger.

Customers scattered to be out of the sure line of fire.

Dutch's hand closed on the rifle, his finger reaching for the trigger, and Jack Burton, with silver flashing from his pistols in the fastest draw ever seen in the saloon, shot both barrels and killed Dutch behind his own bar. He fell out of sight behind the bar.

The secret was preserved.

For the time being.

Stud Carbon, Free from Jail, Bound to Search

After two years in jail for a crime he did not commit, Stud Carbon was freed by a crooked judge who started his own sentence in Yuma Territorial Prison. The judge was also looking for new favors for his comfort, and perhaps his life thereafter behind the bars. *Making Good Too Late* is a crime in itself, more so if it happens behind bars with all kinds of death on the prowl night and day, angels of death, devils of death, oh, Death itself with lock and key making the rounds of internal and eternal miseries.

But death comes in broadest daylight to the wary as well as the unwary.

Stud Carbon, freed by fortune, chance, and new honesty, began to search for the real killer, somewhere out there on the wide grass, in the curl of slow hills settling each and every gaze cast on the horizon. The mission, he realized at first count, might take years, most of his energy, all of his resolve.

But he was bound and bent to it.

Yet the first thing that grabbed his interest, this day of days, was hearing the sound of a train coming around a far bend in the tracks and then, as he let his eyes run over the landscape, he spotted a man trussed to the railroad tracks, one hand and one foot tied to each iron rail shining in the Western sunlight and his body caught tightly between those tracks.

And that trussed man had a black as Hell death rag wound about his eyes, so that he could not see his death coming, but he could feel it thundering at his extremities, could hear it, death never so dark, as this one approaching him, pounding out its odd rhythm, the whole Earth shaking to beat the band, as one might say over a bar top. It was not like a gunfight with bandits or tribal hordes, where both his spirit and his fear might be mounted within him, ready to give his all, his life surely, to the outcome of the day.

Stud Carbon, a newly loosened man, rushed to the figure, not even checking to see if the prospective victim was alive, but to cut him free, his mind forecasting the life of a man, handless, footless, unable to stay on a horse, unable to ride, to rope, to feed himself, unable to survive on his own. The pictures made Stud shiver and shake all over, but surely not with the same fear.

He'd seen many atrocities in his days, women killed, children killed, by accident or by intention, but this was worse than the Specter of Death; this was death itself about to happen in front of him again, this time twisted by brutal hate, a message and a sentence tough enough for the wildest gang to get straightened out, to cut a new trail in life.

Or else.

The earth beneath Stud Carbon trembled with constant tremors as he dismounted and ran to the trussed-up figure, the awful power of a huge black engine of the rails coming 'round the bend like the thunderous repetition of drums upon drums, whole damned legions of drums and their pounding in roar upon roar, all deafening with threats. He believed the Earth itself could possibly be rendered open by such power, never mind the bony wrists and ankles of a man bound, truly bound, for Hell. For a quick moment of imagination, he felt ropes tightening on his wrists at the ends off his sleeves, and inside the comfort of his boots.

He could imagine no crime this big, no sin to be so atoned, no judge to decree such an ending, even as he remembered his own relegation to the quiet horrors of prison, yet able to breathe all the time, able to manipulate his hands and fingers at his whim, measure his way with each footstep taken forward, or backward, at any hour of the day.

Anew, as if warning the Earth itself, the train whistled and tooted a couple of more times as Carbon whisked the knife through the ropes and rolled the once-trussed body away from the tracks even as the engine, slowing down near the sight of the activity on the rails, passed over the spot from which the taut figure was freed from possibly the bloodiest mess he would ever see, bar none other in this life, short enough as it was on its own time.

Men, freed from such circumstances, find alternatives in life, and vengeance has its sway.

The man freed from a certain and crushing death and the man freed from nearly a thousand days in jail, each gasped for their breath as they found themselves face to face on the ground, the train engineer, eyes and mouth agape, staring down at them muttering, "My God man, what was this all about?" He had nearly fallen out the window of his cab, shaken to his bones. In all his days at the throttle of the black giant of the tracks, he had never seen the likes of this event.

The man with ropes still clinging to him in chunks and odd lengths, scraggy in his appearance, exultant at the moment, yelled back at him, "This fellow just saved me from certain death at your hands which had no reason in this, as did he; no reason in the world but to arrive here at this time, as if sent to save me by the good Lord himself."

"Ah, but I did," said Stud Carbon, to the near-dead companion and the near-killer engineer, "I was just freed from prison for a crime I did not commit and am searching for the real killer. I assume the same God who freed us both had cast upon us a bond, as brothers, as boon companions, to form an alliance for the search of the real killer in my case and the near killer in his case." He dropped his hand on the other's shoulder.

"By gorree!!" said the engineer, "By gorree!" He threw his hands in the air and yelled at his fireman, "Did ja hear that, Igoe? Did ja hear that?"

The fireman shook his head in disgrace at the near-crime he might have fed with his own shovel.

At that utterance, Stud Carbon added, "And I swear by all that's holy, my man, that you were sent by that same God to be the witness of our bonding. If you have any words to that affect, dear man of the steel, please tell us." He leaped up to touch the engineer's hand as it swung out the side of the engine cab.

"By gorree!" the engineer said "By gorree, let it be, let it be. I wish I had some gin to bless this bonding, but you are brothers freed from sin. From this day forward, you are brothers freed from sin and I am more than positive that some folks, right from this very minute, have begun to worry what's coming after 'em."

He nodded his head with a solemn nod, as many men in charge do, for self-awareness. It was a signal for movement.

Then the engineer spun about in his train cab and said to his fireman, "Alright, Igoe, let's get on to Houston and tell the whole world this story. Not many of 'em gonna believe us, as they haven't in the past, but something tells me, this time things might be a little bit different. We got a new tune to tell 'em."

He tooted his whistle, loudly and with zest, and the engine huffed and puffed with a series of deep chugs and they were on their way, all the players from this scene.

The Carney Boys

Jefferson and Jacob Carney, Jeff and Jake from here on in, could shoot like Hell, quickly, accurately, deadly is what that means, from the draw to the fall of the target. The way things happen to close brothers, especially to twins, as were the Carneys, assume a remarkable turn of events.

One day, in their 16th year, heading away from home, Jeff continued on the trail to town, Bugle Crow, Texas, and Jake split off the main trail to visit a friendly female at her father's ranch, a dozen miles away, the Al Sheldon spread and he had a daughter named Olivia. He was not exactly a newcomer, but had only been in the area for less than a dozen years, those ties demanding more time on the job, as it was.

When Jake didn't come home that night, the father, Sydney, said, in the morning, "Jeff, you saddle up and go see what Jake's up to. What dang fool trouble he might have gotten into this time. If you run into any ruckus, get word back to me."

When Jeff didn't come back either, Big Syd, with a few of his hands, rode off the next morning to investigate.

Two days later, none of the crew had come back, nor either of the twins. Their mother, Cora Mae, told one ranch hand, "You go into town and tell that sheriff, Roscoe Sears, he better catch up to me somewhere along the trail 'cause there's going to be Hell to pay or some blood spilled, which might be mine because of the mood I'm in." She whacked him on the rear end and added, "Be damned quick about it, Joey, or else."

The sheriff met her at the gulch, on the trail to the target ranch. "I don't know what your boys got going on, Cora Mae, but one of my guys spotted a lookout watching this trail and reported back to me rather than shooting him off'n his perch. Twixt you and me, we ought do our best to talk to him before he moves on. I'm getting a feeling something ain't quite square at the Sheldon place which, by the way, is where Jeff went earlier yesterday in a damned hurry, if I remember."

Cora Mae said, "You've always been square yourself, Roscoe, and mostly ahead of everybody else which is why I pushed for you to get the job. How do we get that spotting rat out into the open?"

The sheriff mused awhile before he came up with a suggestion, or a dare, if you'll have it, for the lady. "It's got to be you, Cora Mae, if you're willing. You, by yourself, can draw him practically off his lookout and down to check you out. Then we can grab him, but you can keep this gun handy."

He tried to hand her a small, pocket-type pistol. "Keep it. Roscoe, I got my own," she said, showing him her .38, shiny, silvery, new in one hand like it had grown there.

Sauntering into the gulch, the walls squeezing up around her, she dismounted, and began to check her horse's hoofs and shoes. She was immersed in the task, as if she was on a stage someplace, when the lookout rode up beside her and said, "Hey, lady, whatcha doin' out here all alone?"

The intent in his voice was detectable, and that building avarice became his sudden enemy as he was surrounded in a hurry by six men with drawn weapons, all of them mean-looking but not jittery, the odds, for a change, highly in their favor. He handed his gun belt to one of the posse who draped it across the rear jockey of his saddle.

Cora Mae said, "You better start talking now, mister, 'cause them's my boys and my husband ain't come back home yet from up yonder." She jabbed her .38 into his ribs, and fear lit up his face, his eyes showing it wholesale.

"Quick," she said, "'afore I really let go with this lonely woman's best line of defense against a scoundrel of a man sneaking behind rocks and trees to keep her in his up-to-no-good mind. You got some answering to do for your scouting and peaking around. What's your name, to begin with and who're you watching out for, by his Christian name, and what're you looking for?"

When he did not reply immediately, she had more advice for the sneak-about. "It's all good on my side, Sonny Jim, if I put a round in you just about heart high 'cause you've been following me and I'm sure any decent judge in any decent court will have sympathy as well as justice for me."

She finished with a blast. "Now what the hell you got to tell me before I change my mind and put my first round right into your privates?" In a flash, her pistol was in that mutable territory, her hand shaking with a dramatic rage, her tongue delivering her rage almost down his throat, his mouth wide open with fear of the unthinkable deed completely in her hands.

He spoke, that threatened man, blurting out his own name. "They call me Curly Tillson and I work for Sam Warrington, who owns the Twin Bulls spread and half of the other spreads in the valley and wants the other half as well. He's got those folks stowed up in a barn on his spread, all of them in irons or ropes, and ain't no way for them to get loose."

When the faint smile appeared on his face, his lips in a half-curve, a nickel's worth of guts on display, Cora Mae slapped him across his face with her pistol. The act drew enough blood to loosen his tongue further; "There's a back door the boss has built for his own escape if the need ever comes. It's flush against some bushes on that backside where horses can be hidden too."

"You saying it's also a way we can get in there if we need to? I can see that and I can see you selling your soul to get out of this jam, but you ain't going anywhere in no hurry, Sonny Jim Tillson, nowhere at all."

Cora Mae had him buffaloed all the way and she knew it.

The reflections of Sam Warrington came into her mind and began to pile up, piece of top of piece, telling the story of a man who wanted more than he had, more than he had a right to, all escalating into a dream about a real land baron, insatiable to every measure, dominance atop a bunch of little people, the poor hustlers of personal energies making way in small way in the big, wide open spaces of Texas.

She had often wondered about a few known transactions between Warrington and some of the early settlers and ranchers in East Texas. Some of them were completed in a dazzling hurry, as if those sellers had been whisked off to another planet, to one of the stars in the night sky, to anywhere out of sight. Her curiosity had never been fully explored, but she now thought a change was due and was coming. In the back of her mind was a whole grave of people tossed under earth and rocks all traces of them lost forever.

And she had never spoken to Warrington, nor looked into his eyes and seen what was on fire there, fire from Hell.

She called one of her hands and said, "Harry, take this rat, tie him up good, throw him across a horse and make sure he doesn't get off our place. Tie him up in the barn and stay with him, you and a rifle. I don't care who makes what demands of you. All he can do now is spoil our chances of getting my boys and my husband back and the rest of our hands. Not for a minute is he to get free of you from now until we're all home."

She waved off the pair of them, saying, "Just make damned sure it happens the way I said." Her pistol waved in their faces, the keenest reminder of all directives.

Then she turned to the sheriff and said, "Roscoe, let's put our heads together and see what and how we're going to get this done. I know you already have done some deep thinking. Let's lay it on the line."

Hours later, the plan studied and rehearsed, duties spread out between whoever or whomever, lawman or otherwise in the gathered allies, the stage was set, and a certain lot of them had assembled beyond the bushes, trees and brush behind the bar. They had been told by the sheriff, "No matter how those guys in there are locked up, secured, remember, everything in iron or otherwise, is rooted or connected to wood, pillar or post or beam, so saws will be handy."

Cora Mae, with the most to lose, and the most to gain, was the sacrificial lamb, a part she had played before without pause, eager to see her family as one again.

So, nearly fallen over on her horse, one of its horseshoes loosened, she drifted aimlessly onto Sam Warrington's spread, a lady in distress from any view.

"Ho, boys!" yelled out Sam Warrington, "Look what we got out here. If it ain't the old pest herself, lady be damned, Cora Mae Carney herself! Let's all give her a welcoming hand, so she can join up with the others, and we can get rid of them all in one big swoop. Then we'll have all the rest of the spreads out there, all to ourselves. We'll have one big piece of East Texas all to ourselves."

In the hullabaloo, in the noise, in the teasing and berating the lady by all Warrington's hands, including the guard inside the barn who had left his post, the rescue group had slipped into the barn with guns, saws, and eagerness, to free the Carney boys, their father, and some of his hired hands from their places of capture, by saw, bars, or odd tools brought along for their necessary use and application.

All went smoothly inside the barn, the prisoners, now freed, were quickly armed and went out the back of the barn to group up as a force to turn rescuers and save Cora Mae Carney from her Situation.

They all managed to move, not away from the barn, but to positions in the near darkness, and all around Sam Warrington and his bedeviled crew in a big circle, all attention on Cora Mae Carney.

You need not to be told who fired first, quickest, and deadliest, with sixteen-year old vengeance to free their mother from her peril, as did Jeff and Jake Carney, cutting loose with a withering fire at Warrington's gang, a good dozen of bad men on the ground in a hurry, moans and cries and curses galore afloat in the night.

At the end of the small war, as the final gunshot was exchanged, Sam Warrington stood alone facing Cora Mae Carney, her husband Sydney and her twin sons, a dark remnant of gun-smoke around them all.

It was the end of an empire in the making, East Texas not quite being what it almost was in another dream, and all of it empowered by a lady of Texas.

The Kid on Three Legs

This kid's name was Drew Jago, soon becoming "Draw Jago," not because of his fast draw, but because he was never seen without a rifle in his right hand, like a cane might be toted by an onery old man, meaning sometimes he might lean on it and thus become The Kid on Three Legs, his due.

To nobody's surprise, the rifle was a Springfield Model 1861 Rifled Musket that now and then carried a bayonet in place, a lot meaner looking than an old man's scowl, for sure, or one from a pissed-off kid.

That's what he was, from the day his father was found shot in the back in the nearby brush region with lots of cowardice-cover at hand and foot, and high enough to hide a tall man, and he'd not seen any man taller than his father's 6'2". In his part of Texas, any man taller than that, he figured, would look uncomfortable on a horse, ride high enough to catch a stray bullet, be seen on the horizon long before he wanted to be seen, the other odd reasons to be imagined, especially by a pissed off kid.

Drew Jago, let it be known right up-front, had gone through the list of gambling pals, card sharks, big-stakes losers from many of his father's table stories, sums often included, looking for a potential enemy, a killer, a backside shooter from the underbrush. There might have been a few stray cowboys who had wandered by their place and acted a bit too brash or unkindly to the lady of the place. And every once in a while, when suggested by his mother while she was hanging the wash, or tending a little garden of vegetables scratching for water and life, he'd ride into Dutch Colony, the nearest town in 20 miles and have a look around, check out any tall men not checked before, his tenacious rifle in hand and ready as ever for the business at hand.

There might have been some out-of-place remark or suggestion from a wandering cowboy that was received by his mother as being too salacious for the situation even though her husband had been killed by an unknown gun in unknown hands from an unknown spot in the low, clinging brush, out if eyesight for apparent purposes, death being another name for the result.

"Ma," he'd ask at such departure time, "did anybody ever dangle odd requests in front of you, cause you disturbance, upset your day's work with their manners, deeds, or foul words of any sort?"

At the oddest moment, just before a retort, there came a shaking about her frame as if the Devil himself had come upon her soul, and Drew thought better of bringing up such visions she must have found anew, the foulest a boy might imagine about his mother being alone and at the mercy of some renegade rider at the door of a widow woman, her story, of course, carried by told tale across the face of the whole region, and who knows how far beyond, about the beautiful blonde living without a man in a lonely place, a woman who kept herself so beautiful and comely that she had to bathe daily in the creek, spend hours at her image, yet be a woman of the wild west.

Some said she rode a horse like a queen was in the saddle, all that elegance really going to waste, the ideas of internal hunger, eternal needs of a woman, being the prime topic in men's minds, a dime'd get a dollar in a bet.

Drew had checked out many of those men to date, the solid good players, the above-board ones, the scaly cheats that seemed to be buried in the woodwork of any saloon, the casual money-in-hand spenders who'd blow it all before the day was over, and we all know that kind and how they stick out on the landscape just like the big winners, like cactus in the wrong place and at the wrong time.

None of them sparked an interest in the Kid on Three Legs, who had an eye keen for suspects, he thought, never jumping at a simply odd or questionable character in saloon landscapes. He figured he'd recognize the difference when his finger began to get jittery on the rifle's trigger, his back suddenly squaring up with interest, to him a sure sign of warning; look up, it said, start maneuvers, a target is now prime on the landscape, it said, on your toes, boy, it might have said. Torment and agony go hand in hand to a boy with the wildest imagination about his mother at the mercy of a world of strangers, for came many of them, for a look, a satisfaction, a glimmer of a hope of chance, choice or contact.

The stage was set in one glance when Drew, in corner of the saloon, let alone by all customer, saw the handsome dog that was Stub Griffon came in sight, a deliberation of entrance at the door, a moment to display regal charms to all those inside the saloon, the presentation of a gift as if the party was now complete.

He was the Adonis of the saddled at the end of his long ride to show his best to one and all.

When Stub Griffon sauntered into The Twisted Horn Saloon in Dutch Colony, for his first appearance in a year, he caught the eye of Drew Jago at that very first moment, how he seemed to lean and saunter through the crowd as if he was really at some other place, and not the saloon. He'd nod at an acquaintance or old trail pard with the merest intent, like old grievances had come to the very front of the meeting, no fondness floating about for a simple grasp, no joyous hellos, or anything of that nature. Like a being at odds from the first look, and him looking like a god must look in the territories of the past of stories told at a thousand trail fires, a film god before there were any film gods.

From a far corner, sitting alone, Jago watched how Stub Griffon sort of leaned his head to one side, a small but detectable manner of evasion he had seen in different men for different reasons, this one being paramount, a stick-out for hiding in plain view; a tall man not crowding the issue of height, 6'7" at least, holding himself aloof and alone as much as he could, a separation being demanded of a crowd.

It was classic to Drew Jago.

He was sure it was murder in person, and right there in front of him and all the others who had shared a game, a table, a drink with his father in those days now appearing to be so long in the past, but mainly the man who had looked upon his mother at the creek, in her own glory and in Stub's glory.

He could feel the tumble of time. How it knocked for entrance at the back of his head.

That old man might never know how much he was missed, unless Drew's own thoughts floated off to the yonder skies, fading like echoes into whispers the higher they climbed.

Every now and then, he'd let go of a whisper, sometimes as simple as, "Pa," as he held the rifle as snug as a bayonet in his arms.

Now was one of those moments that life throws in your path. There were things he could depend on, lean on. He was balanced, ready for encounter, ready for payback.

It was time.

Chaz Brandin, Gunman Extraordinaire

At the first tie-rail in Cougar Hill, Texas, gunman Chaz Brandin slid off his mount and looped the reins of his Palimino over the rail. He wore a tan sombrero, a gray-tinted shirt that showed wear on the sleeves and collar, dark pants of a denim-like material that showed times galore in the saddle. The early sun, almost flame bright, threw his shadow ahead of him on the dusty road. He'd already advised the mayor and the sheriff that he was going to walk down the lone road into town and if anybody dared to take him on, be ready at sunrise.

The message, carried by a stagecoach driver, was not a surprise to folks in Cougar Hill: Chaz Brandin had already announced his entry into six other towns in east Texas, and it looked like he was going to make his way further west. All the way.

Some towns accepted him with silence, not a soul to be caught drawing the line on passage, and the few times a needy hero had stood waiting, he stayed in place, right in place, but face down in the dust, drawing first, dying first, never dreaming of the loss, only the constant saloon-appreciation that was sure to come. Some towns are made by their saloon, some saloons are made by its quick heroes, but neither really complement the other for very long.

The stories had come earlier, from all kinds of folks, those who saw them take place elsewhere, or heard them, even second- or third-hand, because they traveled as if on whispered winds or shouted out in warning: Chaz Brandin was as fast as they come, especially by those who pronounced him as such.

The one difference in Cougar Hills was the sheriff, Patch Hogan, three years on the job, unrifled by talk or mouthy threats, who had seen enough heroes to fill his jail twice over, married to the love of his life, Curly Sims, now Curly Hogan, and the oath he'd sworn never try to be foolish, heroic, or challenged by any awed sort. They all had seen others just like Chaz Brandin over the years, their mouths just as wide, their walk all as cocky as any winner at cards, Aces drawn or beaten, Kings crippled, Queens smothered on the spot before they were enthroned.

That very morning of Brandin's arrival, Curly had said, "The old book looks like it's going to get another page written today. Any special plans?"

He loved the way Curly could round things up in a hurry, but take time to clothe them in a nice civilized way, not say, "Is this to be another day of killing?" She had a bit of class in her morning demeanor.

"No, girl," he replied, "nothing like that for my plans. Let him walk about the town all he wants. I doubt any fool is going to make a stand, and certainly not me, but when he breaks the law, I'll snap the key behind him in a jail cell, and he'll cool off after a few days or a few weeks until the judge comes to town on his own schedule, if he ever settles on one. That man is damned hard to read, even with his hand on the Book."

He didn't rush his morning meal, which would alert Curly to a hidden nervousness, the kind that hung around the corners of her mouth, at the corners of her eyes as blue as the blades on their meal plates, said to be from Paris in France, by a wily old wagoner who peddled to any ladies who offered him sustenance of any kind, including a sip of cool water. "Them dishes," he might have said, "practickly been drug the whole way by wagons like mine, from France, mind you."

The word on Chaz Brandin came to the sheriff in bits and pieces, enough for him to fill his mind and seek the possibilities that lay ahead of him and the tow as a whole.

He heard that when Chaz was not challenged, he went to the saloon and met with the owner and barkeep, Monty Clarke, who stood aside a long rifle laid across the bar, a rifle thin as a rope with a couple of knots in it, and aimed down the center of the saloon at who knows what or whom, but promised damage enough to whatever its slug hit.

"I hear all about you, Monty," Chaz said, "that you're a straight shooter and a man of honor and with a good eye and I don't want any truck with you about my needs. You and me will play it square and I'll pay my own way less'n you offer it up to me. We'll do business together like regular folk. You can stand there with your finger on the damned trigger for all I care, long as we got an understandin' of the deal. It can't get any better'n that from where I stand."

All which sat square in Patch Hogan's mind, and allowed him thinking time so that Curly wouldn't get upset, or him get shot to pieces on some measly misunderstanding.

For a solid week it worked that way, Monty's rope-skinny rifle with a couple of knots tied up in it and laid across the bar waiting on a target.

Then, in a card game getting a bit noisy, voices jumping and yelling seemed like every other hand, one regular cowpoke player jumped up and said to Chaz Brandin, "I saw that! You cheated!" He went to draw his pistol and Chaz shot him dead where he stood and then fell across the table, spilling cards and money all over the floor, and any proof of who saw or did what.

Monty Clark stood with the long, thin rifle aimed at Chaz Brandin, his voice directed toward those near the front door of the saloon, "One of you gents go get Patch Hogan in a hurry afore I shoot the shooter." A volunteer slipped out the door, and headed in a hurry to the sheriff's office.

Chaz Brandin, hands still raised above his head, said, "Monty, we have a deal between us, right from the start."

Monty, in quick response, said, "We had a deal, sonny boy." His words were curt and harsh, and then he directed a nod at a bystander and said, calling him by name, "Jiggsy, you pick up all the cards and count them and tell me how many Aces you find." He levelled the rope-thin rifle once more at the shooter.

The appointed-picker-upper, down on his hands and knees on the floor, collected all the cards, and not touching a drop of silver coin or a piece of paper money, finished is task, and said, "I got 53 cards and 5 Aces."

With utmost ease, as if he could care less about his duties as sheriff of Cougar Hill, Patch Hogan slipped the chains onto the wrists of gunman Chaz Brandin, nodding at Monty Clark, the skinny rifle still at attention, and saying words that Curly would ask to be repeated dozens of time, "Thanks, Monty, you run a saloon as good as any man in all of Texas."

Jess Hardy's Studies of Wolf Packs

Day had swung in on top of Jess Hardy as he listened to the wolves welcoming dawn in their own way, and him never seeing it but hearing them across a lake or down a tight file where a mountain gave up the right of way to a worn path. Never did he see them on that path, bashful, he thought, or not liking the smell of him, or the odor of any man, always accompanied by spent ammo smell, piggery specks that butchers release, cayuse remnants gone to steady pot, every one of them bearing aromas most men never catch hold of on their best days.

His interest in "them thar critters" was established early in his days.

The current lot of wolves, about 9 of them, likely *owned* the territory and he heard knowledge of their tactics and traits from the mountain men he had befriended over the years, each one of those men often suddenly disappearing without a word or a good sign on one of their regular days. It was like looking for one damned egg for breakfast and falling down dead on the spot or getting rushed off a mountain by a boulder on the fly, and being breakfast in reverse order for the very pack that often brought their music to one's ears, at least those that listened alike.

Wolves, Hardy learned from eager listening, were carnivores of good size and range all over the hills of the area, and, of course, much of the mountains of all the West he'd ever get to travel, but they were shy and cautious near gents with guns but, unlike the dog, had never been tamed or trained, "keeping to their own thing," as one mountain man said.

He also learned that they yowled out their music, frightening new folks to the area, and yet were "operatic" to gents like him. He learned from many older men, and from some Indian wise men that there are three species and about 40 subspecies of wolf, according to their wisdom and teaching, in some places, like those tribes which gathered such knowledge over the centuries and were never disputed on any point of interest or information, like "comin' from the horses' mouths being wolves for a word or two." Each one of them, as tradition tells it from the very tongues, were always bound in loose company as young companions sharing some small village compound kept in place by skins and stakes that come in as many different sizes as there are animals for the taking by bow or lance. "One must use all he downs to the last drop. We have only so much coming to us, and that's it."

The most common type of wolf for them was the gray wolf, or timber wolf. Adult gray wolves grew to be 4 to 6.5 feet long and weighed in at 40 to 175 lbs. The gray wolf had mostly thick, gray fur, although pure white or all black ones might be seen in the same pack.

Hardy remembered his interest being spiked by another species, the red wolf, though a bit smaller, which grew to 4 and a half feet, 5 to 5 and a half feet long, and hitting the scales at 50 to 80 lbs.

Wolves, he learned for fact, were found in North America, Europe, Asia, and North Africa. They tended to live in the remote wilderness, though red wolves preferred to live in swamps, coastal prairies, and similar wet forests. Many people thought wolves lived only in colder climates, but wolves lived in temperatures ranging from awful cold to awful hot, like anywhere from 70 to 120 degrees on the regular scale.

The Eastern wolf, also known as Great Lakes wolf, Eastern timber wolf, the Algonquin wolf or the deer wolf, was distinct from Western cousins. Eastern wolves used to live in the northeastern states, but resided as a whole mostly in southeastern Canada. Some folks say that red wolves and Eastern wolves might be hybrids of grey wolves and coyotes.

For sure, wolves hunted and traveled in packs as their way of survival. Packs didn't consist of many members, usually, with only one male and a female and their young. This usually meant about 10 wolves per pack.

A pack's leader was known as the alpha male. Each pack guarded its territory against intruders and even killed other wolves that were not part of their own pack. Wolves, he was informed, are nocturnal and hunt for food at night and sleep during the day.

Wolves, it was known, are voracious eaters and can eat up to 20 pounds of food during one meal. Since they are carnivores, their meals consist of meat that they've hunted and brought down for the pack.

Gray wolves usually ate large prey such as moose, goats, sheep and deer. Normally, the pack of wolves find the weakest or sickest animal in a herd, circled it and killed it together. Wolves attacked and killed domestic animals as well as animals found in the wild.

Red wolves eat smaller prey such as rodents, insects and rabbits. They aren't afraid of going outside their carnivorous diet and eat berries on occasion, too.

Jess Hardy, it is said, began to write much of the foregoing data in a small book of loose pages connected by a clip he made with his hands from odd bits of metal found along the way and which he'd stash away in his saddle bag "for sometime use."

One elderly and local man in Montana said, "I saw Jess Hardy ascriblin' in those pages one time beside an open fire years ago near Missoula in the Northern Rocky Mountains before the snow set-in. I betcha that little pack of words, if you'd come across it somehow, could get you a passel of dough these days, betcha my bottom dollar."

Knot Bretwell, New Deputy

He continued to ride over the crest of the hill, even as he heard the gunfire ahead of him, and that was after he'd not been able to avoid the most prior western music in the air, the ***pop pop, bang bang*** a full day's ride behind him. Knot Bretwell realized he was always riding into trouble no matter which way he turned, which trail looked most promising. Fate might have well sat in the saddle with him.

With that image sitting in him, there'd be no turning around.

There would also be slim chance of avoiding what was meant for him in this life, on this trail, beyond the next hummock of a hill. Fate, like destiny, worked the spurs on his mount, and there was no two ways about that.

This time the combatants were shooting at each other near a small cabin, and one of them was a woman, kneeling behind a pile of stones he thought must be a well crown. The other, a big man, was prone beside a horse, fully motionless, dead to the world and any further riding. The shot that did the horse in was most likely fired by her, and was readily cleared up by her risen voice.

He heard the woman yell out, "You rode in here shooting. It's your fault your horse is dead. You're the one who got him killed. You're not going to get my horse. He's the only one I have." There was no pity in her voice, however, and no pleading and no begging, even if it was her last stand, and on her knees.

Knot Bretwell felt a rush of admiration fill his self.

Knot Bretwell, six days in the saddle, shots shared already on a couple of occasions, figuring he wouldn't miss another single loose round, put that next slug right beside the big man who hadn't seen him yet. He rolled over and looked back at a man he'd never seen before; not a friend, for sure.

The woman raised her hand, waved it at the newcomer, and stepped out from the stone protection. The big prone man aimed his rifle and Knot Bretwell put a round in his back, and a whole lot of bother rising quickly in him.

The woman yelled out, "You did a good deed, mister. He's a bad one. I saw him once before, on a poster, wanted for murder, big as Hell, and mean as they come. He wanted more than water. Wanted another horse for the trail, but ain't going to be mine, much thanks to you. I'm sure, if we bring him into town, Drago Hills, the sheriff will pay you the reward."

"I didn't kill him for money, Ma'am, but to save you from sure death. It was called for, in my mind. I hope the sheriff feels that way about it. I've met some real ornery ones along the trail." He rolled the big man over and studied his face. "There won't be any mistaking him, will there?"

The lady replied. "I'm Harriet Plumbert, widow for a couple of years, and the sheriff has an abiding interest in me, I swear." A glorious smile beamed on her face, as she continued, "and my deepest good thanks to you, mister whatever."

"I'm Knot Bretwell, just aheading west some more, pleased to meet you, and hope you're right about the sheriff."

She beamed back, "Oh, he's in a twist over me, I dare say. Says so himself every time he visits or when I go into town. Not a bit shy about his wants." Her smile was open, real pleasant, no wrinkles in sight, and her hair, despite this recent encounter, sat neat and trim and bore a soft blondness in its tone, as if ready for morn or eve.

Bretwell, loosening up in the woman's company, said, "I can see why," and let it go there. He didn't need any more trouble this day, the sheriff most likely ready for any contention from a stranger and his lady of choice.

They mounted the dead man on Bretwell's horse, and he mounted himself. Harriet Plumbert led the way into town, riding high and proud in the saddle, a sight for any man.

The sheriff, Harry Felixan, greeted them, heard what they had to say, called out to a man passing by, and said, "Henry, we got a customer for you. It's old pal, Trigger Mason, dead as ever. Take care of him for me and I'll see you get paid." The conversation, assignment and business were conducted quickly.

The three sat in the sheriff's office and told their stories.

"Well," Sheriff Felixan said to Knot Bretwell at the conclusion of stories, "would you like a job as my deputy? The job is open, I need a hand, and after I give you the reward money and a badge, and you promise to stay away from Harriet, the way she's asmiling now, I'll give you the rest of the day off. You have any experience workin' for the law?" It was a friendly delivery.

"I pinned a badge on a time or two, but only for a friendly favor, a kind of payback, if you know what I mean."

"Yep. I get you there, a deed done for a deed done. That's good business and good enough for me." He pointed at Harriet Plumbert and said, "and she's outta bounds from now on."

"Harry," she said, if you don't stop talking about me like I was a relative already, I might make a big stink about things as they get twisted your way."

Knot knew the situation in front of him as clear as a gunshot in a rocky corridor.

With his reward in hand, Knot went looking for a comfortable room and found one at the edge of town, on the second floor, windows on two sides of the room, one of them looking out onto the main road through town. He let his long ride fade into the night in a solid sleep, not listening for the snap of a twig underfoot, the click of a cocked pistol, or any of the other signals that night makes use of to ruin deep sleep.

Morning found him at work, the sheriff already at work when he walked in. "Morning, Sheriff. You been here all night?"

"Not quite, Knot." He smiled at his own words. "I'll get used to that." He laughed and said, "We have a shooting just outside of town. Looks like a robbery gone sour but we have to clear it up. One man dead and one man with a pistol still in his hand. You can take the lead on this one, kind of breaking-in thing. I know the shooter but not the dead man, from the word that came to me. Let's go."

Knot spotted the man, sitting on a wood pile, with the pistol yet in his hand, walked up to him and put out his hand. The man handed him the pistol without question or comment. Inspection showed that only one shot had been fired, just the one shot that had done the damage.

"What happened here, sir?"

"I was taking it easy after tending my horses. I have six beauties that everybody knows about. When a stranger, at the edge of day, walks in here with his hand behind his back and his holster empty. I don't do no sittin' still knowin' he didn't come to say hello. I never saw him afore, never once't. And he didn't say anythin' at all. Just went to pull that gun from behind him. I ain't about to let any man swing on me like that, the way he tried, so I shot him. He dropped his gun right where he lays now."

Knot quizzically said, "You only fired one shot."

"That's all it took. I'm a damned good shot."

Knot tossed the Colt to him and said, "Shoot that can over there," and he pointed to a can across the yard.

Bang went one shot and the can spun into the air.

Knot gestured to the man to holster his weapon, turned to the sheriff and said, "Looks kind of clean to me, Sheriff. That other gent had no idea who he was trying to surprise. Didn't even get off a shot I'll bet." He checked the dead man's pistol.

"Still loaded, Sheriff, but I'm satisfied this here gent was protecting himself and his property as best he could, and he's pretty damned good at that."

The two lawmen were riding off, the sheriff saying, "That was pretty clean, Knot. Wouldn't have done it any other way myself."

"What's this gent's name, Sheriff.? I didn't catch it."

His name is Wally Kellogg and we ain't heard the last of him, at which Wally Kellogg yelled after them, "Hey, Sheriff, want me to take him into town to Henry's? I ain't about to bury him on my own property."

The sheriff waved okay over his head and kept heading for town.

The day was a heads-up day for Knot, meeting some other folks coming by the office for morning gab, him placing names on faces after introductions, stories of a sort about long-time connections with the sheriff and, of course, linkage occurring, with Harriet Plumbert, in the sheriff's eyes and plans, instead of saying, "I'm a good friend of the sheriff."

The first argument stared in the saloon, when one man accused another of cheating at cards. He was about to go for his gun when Deputy Bretwell said, "I wouldn't do that for a plain old card cheat, at which the plain old card cheat went for his own gun and the deputy shot the pistol right out of his hand. Bretwell's words hung in the air warm as a promise; "A night in jail should calm you down, mister, and a doc'll tend your hand so you'll remember first the next time if it's worth it all."

When the sheriff heard about this story, he made sure to tell Bretwell, "You keep on gettin' *A's* on the job and I keep gettin' lucky. There's some smooth tickin' goin' on inside you, son. Some real smooth tickin'."

He paused in his delivery, kind of looked back over his shoulder in a deep-thinking manner, and finally said, as if a great learning point in life had been reached, "I sure oughta know now that there's another way to do this job, and better than I ever did it."

In a sudden move, he pulled off his badge, dropped it on the desk, reached for the door handle and said, "I'm goin' out to see if Harriet Plumbert will marry me and have a new top foreman at her place."

The Drifter

Young Doug Bentley, for some reason unknown to him, had kept his eyes on the new hire who called himself Van Tessor, working for his father, George Bentley, for only the second day. Doug let his gaze follow that of the new man as it stretched past the early evening fire on the edge of the herd onto the far horizon hills as they melted into indistinct shadows.

The young man was generally alert to most things about him, but what he didn't know was his father's displeasure, slowly seeping from him, with his general foreman of the ranch and the herds they gathered or generated.

At this moment on the trail, Doug knew the shadows would disappear too soon, bound to sadden him, and wondered if Van Tessor, if that was his real name, felt the way he did at this campfire setting. He hadn't seen other riders, even those who had been around for a few years, show any emotion at all, or any dreams, or even spoke of the moment the way some of them could bring up beans, cooks, or cows only for the sake of breaking silence, bitching about all kinds of conditions, or played on barely being heard, of being here, flat out on blankets spread near the flames, the chuck wagon, the others on the drive.

He had heard one of them say, "That new gent moves too quick, too smooth for me, keep your eyes on 'im. Ever knows, do we, what's comin' our way, even in the ranks, do we?"

"There must be something else in there," Doug thought, letting his gaze return to the slightly dimmer horizon, and "something more to attract him like this."

The intrigue caught him broadside, and made him say, "What are you looking at, Van?" not sure if it was his first name or part of his family name.

The new hire replied, "The same thing as you, Doug. The very same thing." It was immediate association, made the new man kindred.

Scotty Hurlburt, an old hand, said, "What the Hell are you gents talkin' about? I don't see nothin' out there anymore," and truly, as he spoke, the darkness had descended on the far hills. "Night is night," he concluded, and went elsewhere as full darkness came upon them, bedding down, hearing sounds of unseen creatures, counting stars, wondering where day had gone, and taking a bit of its misery with it.

Van Tessor had sort of deliberately picked a spot near him, Doug discovered, as the new man asked, "You got any favorites up there, Doug? Any one of them more than any other, all of them special from where we see them, and only at night, like they're reserved for us by a critter bigger than all of us, like he put them there and he owns the lot of them, head and tail, lock, stock, and barrel, like an old teacher said once back in Pennsylvania."

It was the first time the new man had announced any of his past, a point to be remembered, Doug thought, his eyes finding the North Star, the beacon that it was, the new man in a kind of pact with him, sharing, releasing a harmless root statement. He accepted the joint overture, "on the inside" being one of herders' welcomes.

Van Tessor had only stated the name of the last man he had worked for; Jonas Silberts kept me until I decided to come this way. It was enough for Doug Bentley's father, once in the war-time ranks with Jonas Silberts, "pals, buddies, comrades f'ever."

Doug, seeking this result, said, "Not that He bears watching, but His works do, every last one of them. They circle us every night at first sight, at first saying "we're still here, boys. Even clouds have a way of adding some more mystery to the pot."

"Like taking away and then giving back?" Van Tessor said, as he rolled over, tired, content, bone and mind rest getting some payback.

Sleep, even uncomfortable sleep, was a gift to be accepted, enjoyed, even as the stars went their way in first sunshine, Van Tessor strapping on his gun belt before wrapping up his blanket, as if he was expecting trouble.

Then Doug, still prone on the ground, heard or felt movement or sound from the earth. "You hear that, boys? We got company coming our way."

The camp was alive in mere seconds, the cattle also stirring in the very midst of the herd, two if their own night riders driving horses near the chuckwagon. "Mount up, men, work's acallin' from over the hill." One of them pointed to the east, where a hummock in the landscape offered the closest approach-cover for thieves, rustlers, the hungriest of men.

Blankets dotted the ground as the herd crew strapped on gun belts, boots, saddles onto horses. Most of them had seen, been in such situations before, time to earn their money, protect the payroll that was attached to the delivery of the herd.

The herd began its own stirring, as Doug Bentley and Van Tessor were first mounted and off to the head of the herd, where the strike would come, Van Tessor saying, "It was nice for a while, Doug, good luck and it was nice getting to know you in last night's meeting."

His horse bolted ahead of Doug's mount, as though he had been in this same exact spot before, knowing where the charge was coming from, where the rustlers were headed at the start of their hit: turn the herd, run it right through the chuck wagon area, scatter horses, men, guns into the wild melee, taking advantage of surprise, herd charge, gunfire, thunder and lightning on the hoof instead of in the sky. It was old style all the way, the way it had been done hundreds of times, a quick hit, replacing honest herdsmen with gunmen on the fly.

Van Tessor fired his six gun first, straight out over the lead beeves into a quick start, turning them into a looping curve, driving them toward and into the gang of riders pounding down over the hummock, coming out of their protective approach, firing their own guns, even as the herd, turned by Van Tessor and Doug Bentley, ran at those rustlers rushing too.

It was a stroke of chaos, as the herd rushed into their ranks, the cook on his wagon dropping a steer coming at his wagon, firing again and again and turning the herd from upsetting the wagon, chuck full of goods and food, breakfast for 16 men good and true, if they all got through the ordeal.

In morning's light, the new sun hitting the ranks of beeves, the cook saw two rustlers go down and knew that Purgatory had also come along for the ride. They'd have to bury them out on the grassy plain, a no-where-grave in a no-where-place, no mother setting down flowers, no father wondering where he himself went wrong and when the wicked twist had come upon his son. The old line cook himself could not remember how many such graves he had seen dug, words said of any manner, how men can turn away from quick-dead, quick-dug burials, and then carry on as if nothing had really happened.

Doug's father took matters on quickly, appointing Van Tessor as trail herd chief because of his obvious qualities, and quick actions, also realizing his son had found a new friend who was a trusty one.

He saw quickly how the man-made decisions, so soon after appointment, when he walked one ranch hand to his gear, told him to pick it up and put it on his horse and ushered him out of camp not more than an hour after the new sun was up and working. The new herd chief was aware of the man's inability to do a full and proper job as a trail hand. He had spotted the laggard so quickly it amazed the senior Bentley, knowing a new hunch had been correct on the man's ability.

"Stellar," he said, as if he had never used the word before, and finally figured he had not, not once on any new hire, no matter how far back he could go in his hiring history.

Such observations, as if in deliberate rushes, came to Van Tessor in quick turns of actions, sparking whisper and talk and quick admiration in the ranks of workers, and every man wondering how the new trail boss would handle the off-trail hours, how close he might become to any of them, tight as boss and workers might become.

Probably not any closer than previously, but long-term came into the mix; staying on the job until there was no more job to do. That seemed to be a definite and positive outlook on good men. Yet movin' on was that natural in these days, what with herds, rustlers, mounts, gunplay when needed, a new town with its drawing powers, its saloon, its women in-town or outside of it where a solid woman made her way in the world, and made it special.

Van Tessor, if that was his real name, would be detached from his course by one of those chance encounters, as would young Doug Bentley, older by the minute, older by any encounter.

Just the way things were those days.

Brett Kirkness and the Bandits

At 12, curly blond hair, physically ahead of time across his shoulders and chest, his arms used to work without deep complaints, Brett Kirkness felt ready for the world. He had just buried his parents, killed by a strange gunman because he wanted their only horse.

When another lone rider said he would take over the cabin because he needed a place to live and he had heard the old folks were dead, the 12-year old, rifle in hand, said, "No, you don't get it." He aimed the rifle steadily, no hitch to his move, his eyes on the eyes and hands of the stranger. "This was my folks' place and now it's mine."

"You're only a kid. I can take what I want." He was about to go for his sidearm, when Brett made his stand.

The shot went over one shoulder of the rider, Brett adding, "The next one will really hurt."

The lone cowboy rode off, his mind made up for him by a kid, pride having no part of his departure.

"I'll be back some day, kid. Bet on it." His yell was from a good distance.

He rode into the splattered sunlight across the prairie, the echo of the lone gunshot still whistling in one ear, as if it was going to hang around for memory's sake, remind him of a kid standing his ground. The vision was bound to linger.

The boy, his mind made up, approached a friendly and older neighbor, Drew Jago, who lived a few miles away, and asked for advice.

"I am going to stay at my parents' old cabin, now my cabin and I just want some good ideas about things I should do to keep the place up and running, and it's all got to be done by me. I'm not looking for experienced hands, or any work, just want to make sure all plans are covered, all I need to do to keep it up to snuff." He paused, took a deep breath, and added, "All by myself."

"Well, Brett, I knew your folks for a long time and I know they raised a great kid. They did a solid job. Shows, the way you look for advice, and all that you've done so far. Some folks have heard about that fella you drove off with one shot. Something I'd loved to have seen. The things I'd tell you, you already know: keep water handy, more than you need if you can do it. Keep the wood pile built up, again, more than you need. Keep tools keen and sharp and away from rust. Don't take in strangers unless they're bad hurt and can't go past your place. Make sure your horse is shoed and fed. Get whatever help you need by asking good neighbors. You know them all. And come by any time you feel like talking or listening to an old codger like me." And his added bit was, "But you know you'll never really be alone out here, for sure."

It was the warmest parting he'd know for years to come.

The youngster, all ears, all attention on what the old gent had to say, took it all to heart. His energy went to the care of the cabin, his horse, his tools, and his everyday needs. Did it so well, that in four years, celebrating his 16th birthday with a visit to Drew Jago, certainly older in actions and appearance than at any time Brett had noticed.

"Son," Jago said right out of the blue, "I've written my will and neighbors have copies and my place is being left to you, cause you're like the son I never had and always wanted. Yes, sir, a son of my own." In two months, Drew Jago was found dead at his barn, caring for his horses.

Brett Kirkness, at 16, was a real landowner, a rancher, with two spreads, with six horses, two barns, a paddock, and 10 head of cattle.

And the young ladies of the territory began to look his way.

He started to return the gazes, knew the changes working in him, saw responses, saw interest on the fly.

His adopted dog, Amigo, also a gift from Drew Jago, woke him one morning with a soft hiss and a scratching sound on the bed board.

"What's it, Amigo?"

The dog hissed again.

Brett grabbed his rifle, slipped out the back door beside the wood pile, Amigo right at his heels until a horse neighed from the barn, and a second horse repeated the sound. Amigo bounced across the yard barking loudly all the way until a shot rang out. The dog whimpered in pain, barked again, and rolled over in a frenzy.

The shadow of a man jumped away from the barn leading one of Brett's horses, a gallant palomino, until a rifle shot took one leg out from under the horse thief. The thief screamed in pain, let loose of the palomino who raced off across the prairie.

An hour later, three neighbors, leading the palomino, rode up to find Brett nursing the wound of the horse thief, hot water at hand, clean linen wrapped around a high leg wound, a blanket saddle rolled up under his neck. The thief was recognized by the neighbors committing a similar crime.

"You're done this time, Jackson. You could be hung for this or sent to Yuma. You're damned lucky Brett here has a great shot and has a soft heart, fixing you up like he did. Lucky as all Hell from what I can see, that clean bandage, that blanket rolled under your neck, you still breathing.

That's the luck of the draw for a thief, I'd say." He looked at his pals and said, "Can you beat this," and he clapped Brett on the back and said, "Ain't he something, boys? Ain't he? And he's already got his dog fixed up, too." He pointed at Amigo quietly at rest, looking over the scene.

Brett stood and said, "Jackson ain't done anything. He's working for me and there's no crime done here."

The statement nearly choked the neighbors. "Hell, boy, he's done this before. This time we got him by the throat. He ought to be hung for horse stealing."

Brett replied, "Like I said, he ain't done nothing. He's working for me, and that's that. No more to be said, as I said once or twice already." He patted Jackson on the shoulder and said, "Ain't that right, Breezy?"

Ever since then, Harvey Jackson has been called Breezy, and Brett Kirkness has been a legend in the territory.

The Conquistadors in New Pants

Deek Garcia was in trouble from the first word spoken on the job, a glob of language leaving no interpretation but that of a one-sided son of a bitch who had more hate in his body than a scowl on dead meat. The speaker would never mention Mexico, or border crossing, or any pithy word that said Deek was poor at his work. The fact is, when guns are drawn, an ally's an ally, and he damned well ought to be.

The transplant was a remarkable gunman, quicker than most, deliberate as many, deadly as the best in their part of Texas, as the stories began to conclude. From knee-pants days, his father, realizing some of the future, had trained the boy on the art of survival. For an old man, with one bad arm from a fall off his horse, and one eye just about shot out of his head, the air full of other bullets, he would impose instructions on survival and make them stick like a cow lick on a fancy suitor.

Deek Garcia was a listener and a learner, and knew the language of hate in its merest utter, and let it go the way he did of mean barbs, beautiful bird calls, and busybodies at their useless work; all expendable at gun time. Reaction is a natural conclusion, usually an immediate expression of hate and anger, or thought and temperance, though it is difficult to wrangle them together.

The day he donned the badge of a Texas Ranger, crudely made for him by his father from an old Mexican soft silver and lead coin with a rugged Texas star on the face of the coin, and with a pin attached for wearing when feasible. The badge was Deek's pride after an oath that stuck with him for life. It all started when he viewed a schoolhouse, full of kids he knew, was shot up by a Mexican bandit and his gang, and his life found meaning as the residue of that sight.

It burned him every day thereafter. More to it than a horse, a gun, a badge.

All of this, the current spoiler of words, was fully aware. Chuck Beaurdeaux was Parisian by birth, American by parental transport, Ranger by desire. He loved horses, the wide outdoors not found in New York or Boston, and allowed a series of moves get him to Texas which had been a state since 1845, though the Rangers had been created by Steven Austin another 10 years earlier than statehood.

Things, as one might say, were put in place before him, the road greased, the lane trimmed, yet he was the outsider come inside, and, for these moments, all the way with a badge.

When a new gang, some Mexican locals calling it "Los conquistadores en pantalone nuevos," (The Conquistadors in New Pants), raided in brutal fashion a small outpost of folks, the case was assigned to Deek Garcia and Chuck Beaurdeaux, the improbable pair. Some people thought it was forcing the issue of closeness, others that it was as much a test as a duty for the pairing.

But they responded from the moment of assignment, two men of different backgrounds bound for a kind of hell on horseback, chasing down the new gang, their inner parts and members nameless and unknown from the start. They agreed that lone investigation was demanded of each of them, and without their badges, to poke around sections of the area on their own and keep each other advised of findings and determinations on a weekly basis. That would be confined to a lone canyon, half a day's ride to reach. Both men spoke Spanish, Deek as born to it, and Chuck as a spirited student.

Deek rode into Hollow Springs showing his thirst at the bar of the Horse Head Saloon, gulping down three drinks that made a customer at the bar say, "You look like you been in the desert for a week. mister."

It was in Spanish, as was Deek's reply; "I been drier than desert dust for 20 miles looking for work, and not wanting to hang around the last spot for obvious reasons that got out of hand. I don't like the idea of a noose around my neck either quick or slow, so I went vamoose." He paused, ordered another drink and swigged it down.

The other customer said, "What kind of trouble were you in? Enough for the promise of a neck dance? By the way, my name's Luke Garner, if you're ever looking for me." His voice had adapted a very friendly but inquisitive tone, almost asking questions but suppressing the urge to "dig for info."

They shook hands as Deek replied to Luke's question, "Enough to scramble in the dark, hightail it here to this anywhere in the open country. The fact is that hereabouts looks interesting to me. At least the drinks are great and the company, so far, has been pleasant. I'm in here out of the rain, to say it another way. Both men chuckled with agreeable pleasure, buying each other a new round, and Deek disclosing a quick idea, "Some folks back there call me 'The Storehouse Kid or The Chain Store Kid.'" He was not sure at all where those titles had come from, were in his imagination, but felt they fit the situation with distinction; one of his tactics was hiding small reserves of supplies, arms and ammunition in different areas to be used whenever him or his allies were in danger of being overrun or caught with insufficient means at hand. Some early compatriots even called him "The Grocer."

He had tickled himself. It was an artful way to pry doors further apart with high-falluting claims and stories, to gain inner reaches.

It worked its purpose because Luke Garner opened another door with his reply: "Well, Kid, I got a friend who'd probably be interested in your working for him, and it's all making quick money and having fun at the same time."

"Interests me already," Deek said with honest emotion.

"Well, I'll talk to him for you. You going to be around a while so I'm not wasting my time?"

"No place for me to go now, except to visit a new lady I met on the way here. Damn near held me up for good. Deserves a payback call every once in a while. Nothin' like Chikita Marita for comfortin'."

Their laughter this time was contagious, making the saloon warmer.

Deek got a room, slept off his ride, told the landlord he was going to visit a dear friend, and left early in the morning. Near half a day brought him to Chuck Beaurdeaux sitting against a wall in the shade, his horse tied off behind a huge boulder. He had a smile on his face that Deek could just about read, making him say, "Well, Chuck, you look like you have the kind of news I have, and I hope it blends with mine." He dismounted, tied off his horse, and sat beside his partner, both enjoying the comfortable ease and a reunion of sorts.

Chuck said, "I'm guessing you heard about 'Los conquistadores en pantalone nuevos,' (The Conquistadors in New Pants), a new group of Mexican raiders with a mysterious leader whose name is unknown as yet, but they're as wild and savage as hell and care for nothing but their own gains and satisfaction." His interest jumped when he asked, "Did you hear anything like that?"

Deek slapped his hands like applause and explained, "Keep your fingers crossed because I just might have made contact with a gent named Luke Garner who promised me a possible contact and/or a job with the gang, no name of a leader brought up, just him each time he's mentioned."

He kept nodding, and added, "It looks as good as it sounds." There was a bit of pride in his voice.

"That sounds great, Deek. You got grease on your tongue too, I'll bet."

The laughter was instant on both sides, with no explanations necessary.

They agreed to meet a week later, if it was practical and sensible, successful secrecy being the best for their job, and Chuck promising to check things on his end about any information concerning the new gang of bandits, The Conquistadors in New Pants.

Deek entered The Horse Head Saloon at noon the next day, to find Luke Garner waiting on him. "You visit your friend, Kid? Must be a nice stop-over. Any shares floating around?"

"Not this one," Deek said firmly. "Any of the others are free-floaters and can do what they want, but not my new sweet one." His words were firm, near hard, and said that part of the discussion was over.

Garner tapped the bar top, not for another round, but to say, "Pedro Garcia López, the big boss, wants to meet you, thinks you're the kind of man he wants, that he needs in his gang. Let's face it, force and power are the only ways to get ahead in any fashion these days, a kind of deadly power that makes people quiver and fall prone to harsh demands, and always at the point of a gun, and the more guns the better the catch, the better the spoils.

"Hell, I get a hundred bucks for bringing you into the fold, and he's dying to find out what Storehouse Kid or Chain Store Kid or even what The Grocer means. Says he can't picture any of them and wants an explanation right from your mouth, about what they mean, each one. You really got him interested, Kid. I sure hope you can carry it off. He don't like no halfway stuff, if you know what I mean."

He bought another round, and said, "Tonight's the meeting and no sweet stuff interrupting the session. No visit out of town. Stay put until I pull the two of you together." He knocked once on the bar top to note importance.

A few hours later, in a room at the back of the saloon, Pedro Garcia López made his appearance, gun hands all around him, and he was a handsome dog of a man, a head of curly black hair, a beard trimmed to perfection, eyes as wide as the open trail, a special air about each movement he made as if he was being judged on each move he made.

Neither Pedro Garcia Lopez, nor any of his gang, nor Deek Garcia himself, nor Luke Garner, knew that an odd hand was in attendance in a small entryway where Chuck Beaurdeaux had stationed himself, his attention previously alerted that Deek Garcia was at the crucial point of their investigation. He was armed to the tooth.

Luke Garner, almost at a bow, said, "Pedro Garcia Lopez, I want you to meet The Storehouse Kid, The Chain Store Kid, and The Grocer, all in one swoop." He ushered Deek Garcia forward with some celebrity, his face full with a smile, a hundred-dollar smile. "He can tell you the origin of his names, as only he can tell them."

"Tell me, Kid," Pedro Garcia Lopez said, his face set in an innocent smile, as if he was not about to believe any story thrown his way, "where in Hell did these names get put on such a skinny, rinky-dinky kid like you? I find it hard to believe and don't even have a picture of any of them in my head. You look as healthy as a sick horse; your face shows it."

Chuck Beaurdeaux was ready, two guns in his hands, nerves taught, action at hand, as he waited for the whole scene to explode, somehow realizing that Pedro Garcia Lopez was not about to be taken in by any kind of explanation from a kid with crazy nicknames.

Silently, in his secrecy, he cocked his weapons, palming each move under an armpit, his partner on the firing line.

Deek Garcia said, "Pedro Garcia Lopez, into such lives ordained from the very beginning comes a special dispensation where special talents spin a man through history, balance one's self by gifts never to be betrayed, that are only used when occasion demands the selected person can operate on his special talents to mystify his opponents so that their effectiveness is totally diminished, such as these ways of mine."

And he spun about in a spin and twirl and drew his guns and fired away, even as from secrecy Chuck Beaurdeaux began to fire his weapons with great accuracy, and his spinning, twirling partner fired two deadly shots into Pedro Garcia Lopez, who succumbed immediately and other gang members, in a state of disbelief, dropped their weapons in great disappointment and fear.

As might be said, "The shooting was over before it began, especially for The Kid Grocer and his intuitive partner."

Al La Cazenza and the Letter to the Lady on a Golden Palomino

Alberto La Cazenza spotted the woman on a horse in one burst of golden light and did not know which creature was most interesting, most golden, most lovely, but that woman was riding that horse by herself, no guide, no entourage, no boyfriend. What was she doing alone in this wild valley of northern Mexico, his home country, but certainly not hers?

He had to meet her, to find the introduction best trusted for the occasion, most fitting to the senses of minds perhaps miles apart. The animal, the one being sat upon, was of golden account, like a newly minted gold coin, the shine elaborate, whole, a flight of color lifting off its flanks, off its neck, that mint of such animals best represented by this creature.

The flash of the rider's hair, sweeping unto itself, now and then finding a whisper of wind he could not hear shaking it at him, at him alone on the edge of a mountain as if some immortal being, some god of all gods, had sent her here.

Then Alberto La Cazenza saw a shadowy horseman approaching around a huge rock where he most likely had been watching her, pistol in hand and pointed at the lady on the golden palomino. He stands up, she sees him raise his rifle and send a warning shot at the other rider who bolts back down the trail.

He comes down to see her on the trail. "You ees hokay?" he said, the mimic at work, it seemed, laughter on hold, the stage quiet.

"Oh, God," she replies in a manner that says she's above her audience, "another one that wants to earn money over in our country, but won't try to learn the language. It's a good thing I came down here to teach them how to speak like us. It will be invaluable to all of them." She let go her puffy breath in a flare of impatient release.

It made a point to her audience, she believed, at which she managed, finally, to say, "Thank you, kind sir."

"You teach in Mexico, here?" He pointed to the ground at his feet. "At Mija Tomo? In town? Bes' school here. Ees good, us, you."

Her breath went a-flare again. "What do you do here, in this town, in this valley? Are you a hunter? A shepherd? A guide? Do you always have such quick eyes to see beyond your nose?"

She smiled wanly at that point; no way to go, no place to get to in this conversation. She tossed her golden curls atop the golden horse and was quickly pleased his eyes followed the sweep of her hair, At least, he is aware of other disturbances, she thought, yet afraid it might also be printed on her face. It made her smile inwardly in a fashion.

"Al lead you Mija Tomo, you seet on beauty horse?"

She nodded, said, "Let's hope it gets better than that, Al. Did you go to Mija Tomo?"

"Al too beeg Mija Tomo."

"I'd give it a chance, Al. My name is Charmly Godfrey, teacher, learner, rider of golden horses. My father has a stable of them. Perhaps I can swing a deal for you. We live just over the border on the Giant C Ranch. He sent me to Vassar to learn other things besides Texas."

She laughed, he thought, probably at some long-gone joke.

She confirmed to herself that he was interested in her, the way he seemed to study her and then she put that out of place, the placated spirit set aside.

She spoke directly; "I'm down here to speak at the school and also to hear a local writer deliver an address at the school. It sounds very entertaining and quite mysterious. I have no idea of the other writer, what he writes, what he will deliver. It might be totally interesting." She paused

Her eyes were lit up.

"Al, he try get dere, to school, be found dere."

"It might be too difficult for you, Al. The high language that's promised, from what I have heard." Her right hand was on her right hip, rigid as punctuation.

"Al, he try get dere. Take chance."

She nodded, a prelude to explanation or direction. "Just lead me to Mija Tomo and I'll take care of the rest. But I will say right now it was nice of you to help," thinking perhaps some of her harsh approach might be eased at least somewhat.

He led her to the edge of town, pointed out the school. "I see you dere."

She found a sudden comfort that she'd see him again.

The head of Mija Tomo said, "It is my pleasure to introduce the next speaker who needs no introduction hereabouts, so here he is."

Alberto La Cazenza walked on stage, nodded at the principal, turned to the audience and nodded at them, and his eyes seeking the eyes of Charmly Godfrey. He nodded to her, a huge smile on his face as he said, "I read this," at which he held a few pages of printed pages, very large type size, crushed them in one hand, at which the soul of Charmly Godfrey nearly took flight, and said, without appearing to find a pause for punctuation but which found its own way.

"Ah sweet marrow ganglia matter of mind what inviolable pleasure brings me to my lone typer this time of night in the moonspill mooncream what draws me this way and that from my outer to my inner am I all questions in this mushrooming quiet and dark of night this sound of dead foxes hanging thinly with leaves the den not returned to mother hunted while hunting and dogged down this deep of night this dread of sleeping while my mind can still move its way over the wave of things can extrapolate conjure figment articulate touch smell know once again the musk I could die for right now this instant this eternity for my nares have the memory of fingers and the dry pulp beneath my nails is your deepest residue of love I cannot manicure away lasting Epicurean ashes of these fires.

    I see suck words on lips I see the drip of syllables phonetics of some word rock buried in you as deeply as mine sunless and miles deep past the six hundred miles an hour that our impulses travel from mind to extremities of selves to fingers of satisfaction to fingers knowledge to lips say to eyes move to pits of breast set into teeth like caraway seeds (oh I love the working memory as my tongue worries a pit like a cavity beginning –I form words for you at the touch) what tangible ghost of nights past is near me touching like grass or a spider web not quite there who the spirit travels its hands and lips and words against my ears myself my all as if Chapman's Homer has its speech and touches to me I, I am alone atop Darien this abominable night though I have shares and am shared, oh shared by madness, oh stung by stars and simple grass.

    Oh listen, believe me daughter of words holder of the precious word rock I am just a moonmaster starriser suncatcher burster of cometing yea a farmer plugging word songs but a listener of your night watches walker of your dreams the evil-doer doing done that far thin voice of a star moving on you oh dream death at morning light ah it is lonely the fox is dead I hear the dogs cry above the clash of leaves the horn empties its wail on wind the den not returned to the young wait cold and hungry the burrow walls close in in cool pneumatics the ferret comes slowly at first teasing his mouth waters saliva runs oozing like sperm his back arches he tingles oh love I'd love to come to your mouth to have your lips holding me is volcanic thought furnace-like as though the blade of your tongue is ever merciless why are you so unkind to me why cut memory's cut do my veins intrigue you my capillaries crawl like others crawl except when you loose your tongue you are mad! mad! but I bid you I bid you come at me once all mouth all imagination all energy I would know no other night nor own one.

    I am doomed pusher of thought darer of deeds worder of words I am doomed who such lip when such thigh take the angle of my eye lest I lose that nearing breast bring your mouth where you've caressed use your tongue as gallant blade my private parts to invade I moonmaster master of words roper of stars brander of herds of Pegasus flock beg your tongue talk let it be known beneath your bone I love your curves and wanting nerves sleep comes now just sifting through me pushing its delights into the barest ends of me the torture of a sugar remembered thighs intersect triangle of nerves coming away more slowly than an old rusty sled downhill excruciatingly lovely from the pitch of parting once past time I shot at a doe and oh! I missed! I missed!"

Charmly Godfrey swore later that she had fainted before he was halfway through his talking, most likely directly to her.

Joshua Jenks, Odds to Evens

The west Texas sun had a special shine to it for the first sight of Marla Jenks' new-born son whose name, on her mind for much of the nine whole months she toted him around, was always to be Joshua Jenks come unto her in a dream. Texas, daily, was a hard place to dream but she was adamant in holding onto hers. Uppermost in most minds was daily survival, a knock-down, get-up-quick existence from dawn to dusk, and into the serious night far enough to need dreams to feed dreams.

He was cute as a baby, good-looking as a youth, handsome as a young adult, and fascinated with his father's pistols, hanging on the back side of the door of their cabin, and his horse, his rope, his shovel not far away from outside the door, a cattleman already through several rustlings, two deaths near his herd, threat ever at hand.

Wild Texas on the prowl, much of time spent alongside herds of beeves, horned cows, an explosion of force not needing much to send its power, plight and pulse on a runaway flight, the air a mass of swirling, twirling horns could kill a fallen rider in a flash.

Life, indeed, was many times on the run.

Edjo Evans and his gang of thieves of any and all kinds of other people's property, including a herd of beeves, had reined up behind a dune and watched the Jenks' herd on a controlled and slow procession on a grassy spread of prairie. They noticed the youngest of the Evans' bunch of riders was the big man's youngest son, one known as a kid marvel with his twin pistols.

"Hell," said Edjo Evans, "he's just a big-mouthed little kid who ain't earned any stripes yet to slap on his sleeve. We ought to be able to scatter that herd in a hundred directions. It'll only take fifty of them cows to make it work-up a payday for us, after Jocko gets his iron hot enough for a new brand. He's got a new one all ready for the job. He found a single stray the other evening to give him an idea of a covering new brand. It should all be a piece of auntie's cake for us. We got twenty tried and true hands to do this one." He trained his eyes into the eyes of each man, marking them then and there as part of the pack and bound to do as bidden all the way no matter what resistance came against them. Their oneness was the only manner that could achieve success.

And he went into a series of orders and special tasks that each man was to carry out.

He looked at his best gun hand, a man even he himself could not take on, Joe Seeley, smooth as all get-out with a pair of nearly divine pistols that could carry the numbers of dead results on the handles of both pistols, and simply said, "Joe, get as near the kid as possible and knock him out of the picture. They say the word is spreading about how good he is, but it'd be another smooth win for you. Kids are kids, like you already know, and always lose their nerve or don't know where the Hell it suddenly went when they needed it most."

Hungry for another name on his scroll, Joe Seeley simply said, "I got him." It was a deadly remark of assurance, evil promise, and a sad result for a young cowboy. The elite gunman took out one of his pistols, shined to perfection as though it never had a greasy hand on the grip, never mind the barrel. It caught the sun as strong as a mirror and flashed its speck of light into the eyes of the gathered, and at-attention gang. Every one of them did a solemn and rigid turn-to as if brought to military attention by a commanding general. Knowing and following directions are the tenets of success at any level and any enterprise, including the rustling of cattle from the heart of a large herd. All Texas knew what it cost either way the rustling went, bodies down in the explosive rush of horned animals knocking cowboys from their mounts, or mounts killed in the break-out and their riders ground into the turf of the plains.

Burials would be made in the same hallow ground, often in the immediate area where death had occurred.

Evans' order was taken as the order of the day.

When the gang rushed out of seclusion behind a high mound, screaming, hollering, firing fusillade after fusillade of gunshots in the air, Joe Seeley had his trained eyes on Joshua Jenks riding a solid black mount across the narrowed head of the herd strung out on the prairie, a target erect on his mount, a simple pair of shots would soon put him down. Seeley's excitement rose up from under him as he dug his heels into the flanks of his horse as he drove him in a mad dash toward his target.

Joshua Jenks, long-time hand with twin guns, was armed at the first breakout of the rustlers, and saw the lone rider rushing at his head of the herd, guns in hand, both of them. He crouched in his saddle, moved his torso to a low cross-wise position, both of his pistols on one side of his saddle.

The thunder of fusillades pounded the air, cattle began their mad escape to get away from the pounding in the air, pouring in every direction, high flashing horns commanding exit, cutting into their own members, gouging slow movers, drawing blood, creating sudden bunches of cattle and horns on the riot of slashing hooves.

Double shots from Seeley's guns slammed the air just above Joshua who heard the swift passage.

He loosened both of his own barrels of their rounds and saw the rustler fall from the saddle as a horned demon dragged him down and screaming his last scream as the herd tromped him into dust.

From back along the scattering herd, Joshua heard a screaming voice say, "Seeley's down! Seeley's down!"

It was as if a bugler had blown retreat, or a final warning, as the rustlers, to a man, raced off into the near darkness, just shadows leaning forward in desperate escape for the whole lot of them.

The way it probably turned out was that they'd not meet again as members of a gang and would go their separate ways, no walk-about boasters from their midst nor any of them looking to quickly join a new gang. When best gun in a gang goes down because of a kid gunman, a brand-new star in the making, at their expense, it sure is a ripe time to bury one's head or go prospecting or riding a wagon for pay, any of a dozen escape routines.

Joshua Jenks' mother, Marla, was overjoyed at her son's exploit, hugging him on his return from the successful cattle drive, simply saying, "My boy. My boy."

His father, who had taught him how to shoot, said at an aside from his wife, "Son, you've got the world by its tail, but you have to carry yourself from now on in constant awareness. They'll always be another fast gun looking for a new mark. Be wary. Be careful. They are out there."

He clapped his son on the back, exuberance in its tone.

Sherman "Shakie" Tucker and Golden Mary

He was born a lefty, nervous as a kitten in a dog pound, passed over too often as a playmate, but loved the guns that were anathema to his hands shaking morning until night. From that auspicious start in Calico Flats, by friend and foe came the nickname "Shakie."

It was often said, by parents, friends, or acquaintances, but slightly behind a hiding hand, "In play or work, for jest or job, don't stand near Shakie when a gun is in his wavy hand; that's putting your life in his hand. That's a matter of fool's work."

Successive lines of friends' children had great fun coming up with different versions of nicknames for Shakie, such as Spinhead, or Shaken the Bacon, or Loosie Goosie, or Brain Strain, or Thick Wick, not that they'd stick as nicknames, but it was fun for them at his expense.

In truth, his father, Bingo Tucker, tried to exclude Shakie from friendly visits to or from other ranchers, but Shakie's mother was adamant in her support and protection." He is one of us and he stays part of us. He was made by us and he stays part of us.

On occasion, his father would re-introduce him to a pistol, such as a sudden practice session, to see if time had rectified any of the awful mishandling adventures, but such attempts proved futile, and his wife always reminded him, ""The boy is one if us, Own up to it. He came from us. He belongs to us."

"And you face it too, Martha," he would reply, "that the gun is part of us in this here life of ours in cattle country and I must do what I can to make way for him in this world in spite of the awful chances."

Perhaps, at that point, the man of the family had spoken to God, for somewhere in the ranches around them in Texas, unbeknownst to all that a gifted child was at hand, as there came to another family a young girl who brought with her into this world the heart of a fair mistress, a mind already settled with an appreciation of the poor, the lonely, the misbegotten and the misunderstood. At an early age it flourished so that her family, their friends and acquaintances, even outside chance encounters, observed her makeup and tact at manners of the heart and, indeed, of the harsh parts of the world that spun around her.

Special children get special attention, it's sorry to say, at both ends of the scale.

Her name was settled on her later, after "Sweetie" spent a few years answering that interim call, as Golden Mary at the insistence of her mother, which, of course, came to be "Goldie" for the one and only girl in the family of five brothers. The mother realized "Goldie" was the answer to her prayers, a daughter to balance the heavy dose of male-driven life on a western ranch with beef to be raised, horses to be trained and cared for, and even loved as partners in life: "God bless the man who rides a trusty and beloved mount. He has been provided for."

In her teenage years, known in a dozen towns for her gifts, Goldie heard about Shakie.

"You might not believe it, Goldie, but every other kid his age spends time at tormenting him in a variety of ways. You ought to hear some of the ludicrous names they call him, while his father keeps trying to train him to handle a pistol. Every other kid his age has adapted the gun to his life in view of life around them full of rustlers, robbers, hold-up men of every sort. Some will live and die by the gun, at their own calling. We've seen it hundreds of times."

After hearing about Shakie, Goldie said to her mother, "I want to meet him someday, Mother, so keep that in mind for me."

Her mother understood the root of the request and arranged the opportunity, feeling that she herself was going to be some part of a small miracle out on the wide prairie, for her prized daughter had a way of changing lives where life often changed from moment to moment, encounter to encounter, at dawn to dusk.

"God bless what I have brought into this world and keep her safe and happy but at her given work if that is what she is about."

She could picture her Goldie riding a horse like a Pony Express Rider hell-bent for delivery, being a marvel with the horse she rode as with the people who came into her life regardless of their baggage or problems. Perhaps she rode her horse like Chief Sky Walk rode his pony, as though they had been both born to the saddleless mounting.

One of them, she was sure, would be Shakie Tucker, one of the truly misbegotten, but when she saw him for the first time a flutter ran clear through her heart, for she had seen him as no other person did in all the West. Never had she seen such a handsome young boy who hung his head at the introduction, though he found an instant shine in her countenance, a kind of new spirit in life to deal with. She warmed his heart in the few seconds with her beauty, and owned him outright, as if he knew the difference already in a new relationship. Here was something special, to be now and loved.

In short order, it took over his senses. Every one of them.

She came right to the point, taking a pistol from her bag, putting it in his hand. Taking a delicious hold of his wrist, holding it out straight, and saying, as that hand of hers steadied his whole arm, his hand, his fingers on the gun, indeed, his whole body, "Now take aim at that bucket over there on the fence and knock it to the ground."

Bang! Went the shot and the bucket dropped with a thud to the ground.

It will be like that for you, Sherman, for the rest of your life. No one will be able to shoot like you. Not all the big boasters and big-mouthed shooters who walk about like they own all that they see. Not any one of them, Sherman. Not in your whole lifetime."

He had not heard his name in a sweet vice since his mother last uttered it. He felt special for the first time. And then she added, "Sherman, I will love you for all my life, for you were born for me, and I know I was born for you. And you will protect us forever."

And so, the word on his new dexterity spread throughout the local towns, that piece of Texas, and soon all of Texas.

This all brought, a few years later, one Zip Costen to Calico Flats, entering unknown into The Broken Rail Saloon until he announced his name. "I am Zip Costen, fastest, best, quickest draw in all of Texas come here to meet your half-hearted terror by the old moniker of Shakie, if he'll stand up."

A voice at the crowded bar, said, "We don't know how he never comes in here. Ain't ever seen him come in here even once't."

"Know where he lives?"

"Yup."

"You go tell him I'll start duelin' with some of this crowd if he don't show up to meet me, the best shooter in all the West."

The man from the bar scooted out the door.

Zip Costen shouted after him, "Tell him to hurry. I'm gettin' itchy."

The messenger, Carl Ashton, a friend of the family, was privy to much of what happened between Shakie and Goldie and though he was nervous about the killer gunman waiting back in town to face Shakie, he had little fear of the outcome. He had seen the changes come over Shakie, had seen him knock both jugs and jars and unusual pieces of fenceposts with his gun ability, with never a miss in these latter months.

But those objects never shot back.

"He's a real gunman, Shakie, loud and boisterous and has done this kind of thing a dozen times from what we hear and from what he said in the saloon, and says he'll be waiting in the middle of town to face you. He called you a 'squirt' of a kid."

At precisely that moment, Golden Mary came on the scene, riding up on her mount. She leaped off her horse, wrapped her arms around Shakie and said, "You're my miracle man, Shakie, and the best shot there ever has been down in this part of Texas. Alex Goodsen came to tell me what's going on. I'm going to town with you."

Goldie's hand was on his wrist and as usual the powers and thrills ran between them.

Shakie said, "You're staying here, Goldie. I'll go on and see what this visitor wants of me."

She stood there, as instructed, as Shakie mounted his horse and said to her, "Wait here until I come back." And then he said to Carl Ashton, "Let's go to town, Carl. Let's see what he has to say."

They rode off, with Goldie alone and awaiting the outcome.

In the middle of Calico Flats, in the middle of the dusty road through town, the lone gunman stood at a kind of attention, sudden wonder hitting him broadside with all the differences he had heard about this young upstart, now dismounting about fifty yards away and walking slowly toward him, with apparent ease and not a bit of shaking going on.

"This is not the nervous kid I heard about, not in the least. This kid even patted his horse when he placed his reins over a tie rail, just as if he's coming back in short order. That's not the sign of a kid coming to a duel in the middle of town, all the folks gathered to see another duel in their midst. I ain't seen him shake once and his steps are even and smooth and not dallying and not in any hurry either. Maybe I bit off more than I can chew this time. I wish to Hell I was back home, but here he is still coming at me."

"Hi, there, friend," Shakie said. "I heard you wanted to talk to me. I'd like to know more about you. Where you from? What's your home town?" There was a cheery, friendly manner in his voice, as if it was just outside the doors of a church, quiet and respectful, and not a whiff of gunpowder in the air.

Zip Costen was dumbfounded, his brain almost dead. He had trouble remembering the name of his home town.

He finally responded, "Back that a way, back along the Snake River, yuh, in Hamilton Falls. Yuh, I live in Hamilton Falls right near the river where it dumps off a hill like it's in a rush to get someplace else."

"Well, I'll be a son of a gun," Shakie said. "I been there, even took a dip there."

"Oh," Zip Costen said, "I've done that a hundred times. Right in the middle of the day."

"Well, I'll be again and again. Ain't that something. We ought to go inside the saloon and have a drink with all the boys, talk about Hamilton Falls and the river.

The thought of home came abruptly to Zip Costen, and the taste of liquor suddenly hung in his mouth. "Sounds like a good idea," he said.

"But this gotta be real special," Shakie added.

"Why's that?" asked Costen.

"Because I ain't ever been in there before."

The two gunmen laughed as they walked through the crowd to The Broken Rail Saloon, four hard irons in place on their hips, not a scent of gunpowder in the air, nor any ugly echoes of death.

At the edge of town, Golden Mary stood in continual silence.

The Passage of Apollo Greysmith

It was not an easy start for newly baptized Apollo Greysmith, his young mother, Verna, thrust into a maddening frenzy right after the trailside ceremony and the conferring of his name. Apollo disappeared almost at the same time the wagon master gave the command to "move out." Verna ran about hysterically and her husband and a few of the ladies had to settle her down as much as they could while the hurried search went on.

"Perhaps one of the younger girls borrowed him," joked her husband, Jeffrey Greysmith, as he scoured the area where they'd stopped for the evening, aided by some of the fathers. "They've been showing him so much love and care since his first hours. They'll be there with their own child or children before they know it," he said, projecting a quick and serious nature. "Yesterday jumps out at us in a damned hurry; we hardly see it, we have so much on our minds, so much to do. That birthmark on Apollo's chin doesn't even faze them; at least not the way it first hit me and his mother."

The look on his face was portentous, fearful and suddenly innocent, as if nothing untoward had actually happened, while overhead, but at an angle as if Boston or New York was pushing it from back east, the sun rode well into its orange blaze atop the Kansas territory.

Time, too, was on a journey; was his son Apollo now on a journey, one with an unknown destination? How would Verna really handle this? How could he?

The newborn in the long hours that followed was not found and the parents stayed behind in the general area, with three volunteers, as the wagon train departed the overnight location on its trail westerly. After searching for a whole day, the volunteers left, but the parents remained in the choicest part of the area, knowing their own lives were at risk as long as they were not a part of the collective force of the wagon train. They became a lone remnant of the long column on its way west; they were, supposedly, alone in formidable country, their child stolen, eaten by creatures, perhaps reduced to the softest of bones.

Kidnapping had not entered Greysmith's mind, not here on the wide grass where you might see a horse or a buffalo a mile away; it was unthinkable that someone would steal a baby.

The search was useless, frustrating, not a sound heard, no whimpers or cries of a lost baby, the wide sweep of the prairie holding back or hiding everything that could lead to discovery. Not a single sign lead them any place, as if their child had just been swallowed up by a cloudy mystery or a mysterious visitor. But even then, the possibilities, the doubts, the realizations began to form, shape up in his mind, begin to reframe his attitude, his character, emanate to his energy.

But, in a like mode of thinking, it was logically surmised by Greysmith, that whenever and wherever his son Apollo might be sighted, from the day of birth and forward, he'd be recognized by the outstanding birthmark on his chin, a triangular birthmark as if it had been sunken or dyed in deep red by an artist, by an architect, by a God with a plan of vengeance or retribution of past deeds. And he had begun thinking without sharing his thoughts that there was a reason enough for the mark to have been left on his son.

More than one person, in short order we will see, came to that same conclusion.

Vociferously, backing up that vein of thought, some of the wagon train youngsters, because of the unmistakable shape of the birthmark, had been calling him Little Tipi or Wigwamy, the mark looked so much like an Indian tipi, even to the poles as if emerging at the top of the fire red tipi, and the silent, open but shadowed flap carrying a mysterious message with it.

So much did it look like an Indian home that a lone Cheyenne scout, called One-time Look (*No'ka-he'konenóno'e*) by selected name, crawling around on the plains grass, keeping track of the wagon train and its people, totally interested in and curious about the white people of the column, saw the baby with the strange birthmark. Immediately, knowing it was a special mark delivered by the gods on high, he kidnapped the baby near a thick mass of brush when the mother turned her back, hiding for two days in a cave hidden by another clutch of dense brush.

Later, after being passed over dozens of times by searchers and under cover of darkness on a cloudy night, he took him to a Cheyenne mother who had milk for the child (*néstovohe*) (*vai*). They both exclaimed about the mark and knew it meant that a messenger to and from the Great Spirit had come to the Cheyenne with the distinguished infant. Perhaps, but most likely, by way of *Maheo* or *Weeho* or the dreaded *Ma'xemstaa'e*, messengers from the great one residing high above all life, all things, even the stars and the moon in their endless and fabulous voyages, longer than the otters swam the long rivers or the moles worked through the heart of Earth, longer than the wild and beautiful horses that had come upon the Earth from the great curve below them where the waters were wide and warm to the touch and not from the top of the Earth where the waters stayed frozen forever, like the old people said.

One-time Look was not only a superb scout and tracker, but so well-versed at a young age in the history and customs of the Cheyenne that he was considered a coming shaman while already known as a brave warrior and scout. In addition, he was touted as *Kahuna* by the tribal elder who knew he sometimes entered trance states during rituals to practice healing of a kind along with the tones and chants of divination. When he was on the trail it was told that he was empowered by the Great Spirit to see and reflect on divine or other-than-worldly matters. Red Porcupine, who as a young brave gave half his foot to a great rock on the mountain, once said in his own language words that meant, 'One-time Look sees where the brown bear walks and where the black-tailed prairie dog (squirrel) puts down its paws. If he doesn't see the tell-tale marks, he smells them or hears them after they've passed his sight. His eyes see you after he has gone by your place of the day.'

Such a matter was the identification of the white baby with the red birthmark as a messenger of the high gods. Other white people, taken or found, lived within the tribe and had become settled in their predicament after a period of time, especially children who integrated with Indian children and mother figures.

June it was, month of The Fattening Moon to the Cheyenne nation, and on occasion One-time Look, out of a driving curiosity concerning Alights-on-the-Cloud's (*Vaiveahtui's*) natural parents, kept his eye on them and realized they were making plans to settle in the immediate area. Soon, on the flattened rise above a wide stretch of grass, and near a small stream rolling off to the nearest river, the man of the family started building a small cabin, his wife planted a small garden, and began hauling, cutting and piling firewood beside the cabin.

A homestead arose in the wilderness, but there was no child to share it, to create love and laughter for the soft hours.

As One-time Look knew the English, he understood what Alights--on-the-Cloud's parents said when they hailed each other at tasks. He knew they were not leaving the area where they had last seen their son, would not leave even though they faced innumerable dangers in this formidable place.

They were digging in, building up, becoming part of the land of the Cheyenne nation.

One-time Look, after a few months of scrutiny and study, realized that their wood supply would give out before new leaf's time. He left tracks in a selected area where half a dozen blow-downs were visible, along with standing dead trees, and scattered limbs with decent thickness, all those with good wood, where the man would find them and haul them away, like gold from a mine. Included in that gathering of wood were several squaw-pine limbs he had pulled down with the assistance of his horse and a rock tied at the end of a rope and flung up and around a dead limb waiting to be drawn down at pressure's call, just the way Cheyenne squaws gathered firewood.

Once, taking away the last of the logs he'd split from this arranged source, Jeff Greysmith sat his horse and studied the territory 'looking for the hand of gifts and not the gifts of hand.'

It all brought him up sharply, slashed into his reasoning, opened his mind. What was working here he did not expect, could not explain, dare not explain. His own horse acted queerly, as though it too looked for explanations. Was it true what he had heard about horses, that they have other senses? If he let the reins loose, could Big Chauncy find his son? Or find what seemed to be lurking in the shadows, in the brush, or exist as part of the Earth itself the way a fallen log lies that once had been the trunk of a living tree?

He wondered if he should tell Verna that he thought all *this* had something to do with Apollo. His heart near burst with the thought and the possibilities emanating from his feelings. He thought he'd best keep such thoughts from her, the possibilities being wide-spread, enormous and yet ominous.

She took the sense of wonder away from him. "You're like a machine with that firewood, Jeff. You're catching up to Winter as you stand there, but I know you're not really standing still as you stand there and not for long." She hugged him and he knew again a slight twist of hope, but said nothing of his suspicions.

The pair were so busy otherwise with their home being built, along with necessary survival duties, that they spared little time for wonder and worry, though they never settled on acceptance, final acceptance, of their little Apollo, a fertile and growing memory around them as every gentle twist of a tale brought new memories into their triangle of love.

One time, the sense of a tear floating in the blue-green of an eye, she said, "Remember how he wrinkled his chin and it looked like a flap was opening on his tent." Much earlier, Jeff Greysmith realized that she never referred to the birthmark as 'the tipi' but as 'the tent.' Such little admissions, such little recollections, made the situation bearable for him and often sparked his energy with sudden drives more than the usual. Though such conceptions and hopeful ideas might remain unobserved by a casual eye, they became dependent upon one another for such lifts. Greysmith swearing at times that a day every once in a while was a day bringing discovery closer to them.

As it was, in the Cheyenne camp, where Apollo, as we know him in one connection, and as Alights-on-the-Cloud or *Vaiveahtois* in a second connection, the infant was becoming a focal point of attention. This had all been foretold to One-time Look by more than 'one voice' and at 'more than one time.' And the Cheyenne 'mother' said to a gathering of maidens and mothers, "This infant has come to us from the Great Spirit and the Gods of the Prairies to suckle at a Cheyenne breast. What great honor has come to us and what great joy." The twinkle in her eyes circulated widely in coming days and her own sworn brave gained additional honor himself.

Events unfolded in small and large manners, and each one heralded the new history that was being written in the lore of the plains.

It all came to One-time Look's perception that each time a cloud came over their lodge or village and at least one young Indian child was near *Vaiveahtois,* and grasping his attention, that *Vaiveahtois* pointed out some nearby and visible object, landmark or creature. One-time Look understood that a new name was being cast from the clouds on high, from the God of the Clouds and the name was being conferred by *Vaiveahtois.* So named in this fashion was Bear's Head, Tree-with-Horns, Gray Bark Swims and many other names that were new to the tribe. *Vaiveahtois* never gave a name to a child that had been previously used in the tribe.

These significant revelations to the elders of the tribe further entrenched both One-time Look's and *Vaiveahtois's* spiritual positions, and responsibilities, within the village, within the tribe. They became a confirmed brotherhood in the eyes of the elders, the elder brother and the younger brother, each with special gifts from the Great Spirit.

At strange moments with strange announcements, On-time Look was advised, told, warned that his trance time was approaching, making headway into his consciousness, taking over his mind and therefore his body. He and others thought it was the influence (or the intervention) of the little white baby with the vivid red mark on his face. It brought a stream of words, a sense of music, a variety of objects, places and conditions to his awareness. Was any of it real, he wondered, and how far would it go if it was real? There were times he could not bring back some of the scenes that came to him in such periods; could *Vaiveahtois's* influence work that deeply on him? An infant? This white infant, when the land of the Cheyenne was, in effect, being invaded by wagon train after wagon train, by clusters of folks moving west, by noise and guns and the thunder of thousands of cattle moving where the buffalo had been so free?

Was he free, himself? Was he too tied to this baby, to the parents? Did he owe them?

He was aware now, this minute, that he was caught in the arcs of life, the full range of them as they spoke to him, brought all his world to view, parts outstanding to him: The moon serves the stars, the dead oak still leaning at the bottom of the foothill, the memory of a dead girl at the foot of a fall, leaves of autumn rushing through a dry valley, the wild spotted horse in the north country of the Nez Perce that carried a name he could not remember but dreamed of a hundred times, a white-boy child's red mark to be carved all his long life, his own hearing atop the silence of the earth when wind and breeze and the wafted odor of his own self just as the elder looks to him for a new name on an old thing and the words come from elsewhere. Does *Vaiveahtois* hear the names even as he points a finger, a stubby arm? How strange this association, as well as the need, the overwhelming desire to protect the parents of the infant that suddenly rose in him like the bond of a brother. Why did this rise: does it ever end, bring calamity with it?

When One-time Look came out of his trance, the elders were staring at him, wide-eyed, stiff as atones in the presence of the young *Kahuna* caught up in his own magic. None of the elders were aware that his gaze was also on the natural mother of the child and the understanding that came to him that she was reacting to her loss in a way quite different from her husband who buried himself in work and search in the same breath, never refusing to check on the slightest lead. The father remained robust, alert, a true seeker, while the mother, he heard hailed as Verna, began to sink into a spiritless state, sadness riding her like a pony from a long ride across the desert. From many vantage points, as he studied her behavior, he wanted to ask her if she could speak Cheyenne by simply saying, '*Nétsėhésenėstsehe,* Do you talk Cheyenne?' But her actions and attitude said it would frighten her into a severe reaction.

He held back on any approach, hoping she could work her way out of this sour state, but each observation convinced him that she was tending toward serious action, depression, destruction. How unfair that would be to her gifted child (even with her own loss in the matter), and to her husband, and to her even as the Great Spirit might see her as she really was.

Twice One-time Look had seen her go near the bluff over the river, as though she was in a dream. His mind flared with the possibilities and the Great Spirit was talking to him, trying to make him speak out, to say '*Nóxa'e,* Wait. *Névé'nėheševe,* Don't do that!' And when she seemed desperate enough in her reactions, the Great Spirit upon him, shoving him in her direction, the commands almost inaudible, hidden from immediate reasoning, he rushed at her as she was about to jump off the bluff into the water far below, throw herself down upon some picket of pity, gore herself forever on her loss, and as he ran on his mission he shouted the words in English; 'Wait! Don't do that!' In mid-flight he caught her hand even as her husband off away in brush, himself leery of her condition, saw the pair of them jumbled and tumbled in the air and then hit the water.

Greysmith had his rifle in hand, fearing he had lost or was losing his wife, but he'd get the Indian that tried to kill her, was trying to kill her, and she had been so severely depressed since Apollo had disappeared. Was she, in her depressed state, involved with an Indian? Had she been cheating on him while he had been working? Was this how firewood was found in a mysterious manner? The questions piled up on him. Was she pushed? He saw no others about the bluff. No other Indians except the one now with his wife in mid-air, clutching for her, reaching. In his chest his heart felt the pain of a double loss.

He'd aim his rifle ... but at what? Was there any point to going on, getting past this? But where was Apollo?

Then Greysmith saw a strange sight in the turbulence of the river ... the Indian trying to save his wife. She seemed to be fighting him off. Her head went under the surface of the stream, came up, went under again. The Indian dove immediately after her, brought her up again. It was all crazy, difficult to look at. Why had they come west? he questioned himself. Had she been against it? He couldn't bring back an argument. The Indian brought her back up again as she continued her destiny's decision, not westerly but deadly.

Greysmith, stiffening his resolve, his hope, his tried faith, rushed downhill and came to a bend in the river where he awaited the pair coming downstream, her continuously fighting for her life, the Indian helping her while being fought off, the waters splashing about where there was no rough water, no rapids where the white of his wife clashed with the red of the Indian, where the opposites, at a glance, contended.

With difficulty, One-time Look brought her to the bank of the river where Greysmith had placed his rifle on the ground, loosed his gun belt and also dropped it on the banking and rushed into the water.

The two males managed to get her ashore as she gasped for breath, hugged her husband, stared with wonder at the Indian whose face was deeply scratched, where blood had run from onto her clothes.

One-time Look made the offer in English to the Greysmiths, "I have seen you search for the child with the red tent on his face. I will find him for you and bring him to your arms." He was speaking to Verna Greysmith, now recovered from her awful and dire attempt at squeezing the life all the way from her body, where little of it remained after her son Apollo was lost.

"I will travel two moons with you, leading the way west with the sun as it chases us, speaking for you all along the way through the Nations, but you must take Alights-on-the-Cloud far away from here. He has landed as special among my people, the Cheyenne, but he is a gift that the

Great Spirit gave to you in the beginning of his time on Earth. I know he best belongs to you. There is enough sadness out here on the wide grass and He tells me more is coming this way."

For the one and only time they were in his company, the Greysmiths saw deep sadness descend on One-time Look's face. Jeff Greysmith assumed that he was looking at the future directly in the face.

He looked over his head as he spoke the English, as though asking forgiveness, "I took your son from you and I will bring him back to you, but you have to be ready to move on as quickly as you can, like a prairie rabbit running from the hawk."

The Greysmiths had one chance and it was with the Indian who had stolen their son and started all their pain. Now he promised to bring Apollo back to them and they would leave their new home.

At the Cheyenne village, one elder noticed a strange mien about One-time Look, how his head kept dipping, his eyes averting his gaze, and realized that the young *Kahuna* was in *another place* for the time being. He did not know where that place was.

He found out soon enough, for a cry went up that *Vaiveahtois* was missing, that he had been sleeping and now he was gone, as if he had crawled away.

The sky turned into a sudden grayness, then a stormy blackness took over all the way from one western peak to an eastern peak, and then thunder and lightning ripped across that upper sea of darkness until the whole world seemed upside down.

The elder, in deference to the young *Kahuna*, entered his lodge without a word uttered, turning his back on what was happening all around them.

One-time Look, carrying *Vaiveahtois,* Alights-on-the-Cloud, Apollo Greysmith, slipped from sight and was out of the village and on a dead run for the Greysmith's cabin a dozen miles away. Apollo, of course, never understood what was being said in his ear, "Momma comes. Momma comes. Momma comes." He said it dozens and dozens of times as though he was preparing the infant for re-introduction to his birth mother, but, in his own way, in the way of his people who were making amends, he knew the words were being delivered by the gods of the winds far ahead of him, down through the valley, across the sea of grass where the eagle and the hawk and the buzzard soared in turns overhead, past the canyon where the coyote had greeted dawn before darkness disappeared, and along the river where secret eyes set on the eyes of men, toward the uphill rise and the small cabin sitting alone like a sentinel's post, eyes continually cast back along the trail and filled with expectation ... One-time Look's promise working along with the gods of all the Earth and Sky.

One-time Look learned a new word in English, one he had never heard before, but whose meaning he understood without explanation from Jeffrey Greysmith when he exclaimed, "Ecstasy, One-time Look. Pure ecstasy," as Verna Greysmith, her depression vanishing in one great bound as though her body had been emptied and refilled with happiness, hugged her infant son, who might have been lost forever, tightly to her breast. Then, motherhood all tightened up in her as stiff as old rawhide knots, dared feed her baby son in front of a Cheyenne brave ... all to make up for lost time, to say what could not be said.

The three adults finished loading the wagon and set off for the farther edges of the west, led by a young Cheyenne brave who stayed the whole of two full moons with them through other Nations.

It was understood by the three adults that they traveled as a family, which would soon break up one more time, long before they reached their destination.

Neither of the parents knew what the infant knew, what Apollo Greysmith, Alights-on-Cloud, *Vaiveahtois,* was bringing with him; maybe he'd never know.

No'ka he'konenóno'e, One-time Look (hard), was told from above that *Vaiveahtois* would never forget what the Gods had given him, and what the Cheyenne first saw and gave to the future.

But the deep debt was due and payable.

Tracy Kurt Elbert, Bumbler by Birth

TeeKay Elbert started off on the wrong pair of feet right at the beginning, missing his due date by a month, catching his mom and dad on the trail, Shoshones and cattle thieves all around the territory, interaction wide open, with real guns and real bullets. The worldly debut was auspicious if not a marker for the years coming down the trails toward him.

There came an immediate notification to others around him that he was short of good sense and good judgement, as well as good execution at the easiest of tasks, therefore a delight to pranksters, bullies, name-callers, other mean slobs lording over the incapable, the impractical dummies, as they said, hanging around for no good reason. "He'll be useless his whole damned life, and a burden to whoever stands by him," was said and believed by all such maligners of the weak.

What none of the teasers and bullies knew, hidden from all as if on a mission by TeeKay's elderly grandfather, Isaac Elbert, bearded, worn, wearing down each day, a figure of the old West, were instructions concerning command of a special rifle. It was a Springfield Ought .56, to which TeeKay, by slow but steady application and further nudges and demands of the old gent, found the single capability to come to his bumbling person, and a deadly shot if there ever was one, enough to keep him sane and dedicated to survival whenever demanded.

The upshot was TeeKay became a dead shot with the Springfield; all he needed was a simple target. Empty tins, dangling branches, scurrying snakes and such ground creatures, were easily accounted for, but none stood tall as a man bent on a lone mission. Such, as fate has its ways, came with a boast by a local big-mouth, Brud Burden, that he'd get TeeKay's place of residence, a mean old cabin on a small spread, as his personal new home. His wants were tantamount to acceptance, take-over; wishes made, wants supplied.

"It'll be easy," he told compatriots; "I'll just scare the Hell out of him, he'll bolt for the wide grass, and I'll have me a new home for my bones at day's end."

Those compatriots took him at his word, counting on a new hangout for the lot of them.

Yet even the smallest history has a start someplace along the stretch of days, or there's no Day Two.

As it was, without any great surprise from a youngster, with a shiny Springfield Ought .56 in his hands, the face-off was limited by the nurtured guts and confidence of TeeKay and the limited size of guts down inside the big-mouth, slowly and surely moving away from the target zone, wise decision no one else might have any need to know being his hope.

All of which, of course, was big-mouth's hopeful secret, lasting less time than a coyote chase. It seemed that everybody in creation, being that part of Nevada, had heard about the stand-off. As one old Nevadan said, "I think we have seen the beginning of a legend rather than the end of one." Brud Burden did not hang around much longer than a forgotten joke after a card game. *Kaput!* Out of sight, out of mind.

The years passed, the shootings scarce but ennobling, and when a huge cattle drive was completed and the cattle train, loaded to the gills on every flat car, moved eastward from TeeKay's hometown of Bugler's Hill, to a huge market, the air was suddenly bound to be full of ideas and festivities, a jamboree, a rodeo, a bull-riding contest and like attachments, broke out upon the land. The crowds came from all over the hungry West, the card sharks, the ropers and riders, the ladies by droves of course, the cheats and the wait-to-be-cheated came, the full-time hustlers of the innocent, the innocent themselves, all came, those crowds came, the seekers, the do-ers, the good and the bad in a mix of merriment, challenge, take-or-be-taken, soon reigned on the land itself.

There came arguments, disagreements, skirmishes by the dozens to be truthful, the town fathers realized there had to be a temperate soul put in charge of the safety of the town, those visitors, the sweet, the sour, the in-betweens. Even this meeting, called in a hurry, had its own arguments as efforts were being made to arrange safety and protection as a rule of law and order.

It was a good thing that TeeKay's grandfather, elderly Isaac Elbert, was not in that meeting of town fathers when one of them banged the gavel on the bar top and screamed aloud, "I appoint the dummy, Tracy Kurt Elbert, Bumbler by Birth, to be the temporary sheriff of Bugler's Hill. He would serve as our major voice of conduct, and if he were to be ill-considered by this massive crowd, we'd not be hurt in the end by any real problem that he could or might take care take care of with his steady aim on that rifle of his. He's the perfect *Patsy* for us."

Came a moment of silence as image and imagery floated in a mix of air with debate on the appointment a surety.

It made him more explosive.

He banged the gavel again and again until he had the mob of them under his wing and sway, and he yelled aloud, "Someone go get TeeKay so we can swear him in. Better now than too late to get it done."

TeeKay soon stood before them as the loud one said, "Tracy Kurt Elbert, we the town fathers, after due consideration, appoint you as Sheriff of Bugler's Hill through to the completion of all festivities. Do you accept this appointment?"

He held aloft a shiny, starry badge as a signal of the new office.

A keen silence reigned in the saloon, as TeeKay said, "I do," his eyes lit up with a sort of instant glory and acclaim took hold of him.

The saloon crowd went crazy.

TeeKay, the badge prominently displayed on his chest, walked out to observe, with a new view, what his town looked like.

The first man he met outside was a former childhood bully and teaser, who yelled out to the passing crowd, "Look who the Hell is our brand-new gaudy sheriff, TeeKay the Bumbler. What the Hell is going to happen next around Bugler's Hill? Are we really in for it?"

His hearty, ages-old laughter, gathered for a moment a sudden sense of bewilderment, until a round from TeeKay's shiny Winchester roared beside his head in the loudest retort he had ever received from any of his bully's words.

It was conclusive, that single round. He was stunned and locked up in irons before he could take a deep breath, TeeKay grabbing two men and saying, "You are now deputies and will lock this man in the jail until the judge settles the issue, I think."

Doubt galore grabbed the pair, but the quick appointment worked its wonders as they marched off to jail with the newest prisoner in Bugler's Hill as directed by the new sheriff of Bugler's Hill.

The story of that encounter passed through the town and all the crowds gathered in various venues, until it came to the old man of the West, elderly Isaac Elbert, who simply nodded in appreciation of his small but insistent part in the heady drama.

Twenty years later, Isaac Elbert down the trail for a dozen years, Tracy Kurt Elbert, Bumbler by Birth, was still the sheriff of Bugler's Hill.

Joey Charlo and the Big Black Bear

When prospector Joey Charlo built his cabin in front of a cave on Colorado's Flake Mountain area, he was planning to spend a year in the area looking for his dream cache. After checking out the cave as far as he figured he needed, he saw no signs of habitation and figured it was a good spot in case of an emergency. Life, he thought, had few sureties beyond the next dawn and possibilities were highly imaginative, but necessary.

There were several other prospectors nearby, most of them friendly, some of the cussed variety, one of them, hurt years earlier from a fall off his horse, sat chipping away at a rock wall as though he was looking for a way through. He never smiled and nobody cursed him for it, life itself having strange trails of its own.

Once on a rare rainy day, Joey decided to check out the cave a bit further than his last such visit. He still found no recent signs of habitation and wondered about the situation. It was at such times, when he was alone, that he agreed to talk to himself to keep a sense of company.

"With the first look around here, a gent would figure a whole tribe or a clan could live here for ages, there's so much room and a sure way out I ain't found yet, me and my miles of hunting. Some folks you meet sure have a way of disappearin' at the last minute, knowin' they was goin' all the time."

This recent search, really only 30 yards or so more than the previous exploration, earned from him the new moniker, "The Long Haul to Nowhere." Surprise hit him for his ability to bring up the new name, which he really liked and made him content on another day without a strike at an exorbitant treasure. "It ain't every day a man has himself a small treat of pleasure. Hah, *The Long Haul to Nowhere* sits well in my mind. I might as well share it with some of the boys. He practiced the recitation on the long way back to his cabin.

When he got back to the cabin, he forgot what he had created, but found that his cabin had been entered and mistreated by someone or something. He set about to clear the place up when he found excrement proof that a bear had been the visitor. "Oh, crap," he said, not realizing the connection, but aware that the cabin door was not even broken by the entrance, and said clearly so he could understand it himself, "I'll have to spruce it up, or pie it up, or oak it up before I get to sleep tonight."

He had realized that he was not really put out by the visit or the mess because he was in black bear country to begin with. "They was here before me," he managed in his humility of man in bear country.

That afternoon, the rock chipper, on a quick holiday, came for a visit. "I wanted to tell you, Joey, that I saw a big black bear open your front door like he's been here before. I sure stayed away from that big fella the size of a giant spud havin' lots of eyes." He laughed at his own joke until Joey joined in like they were a duet at a stage show.

"You sure bring some fun atop the bad news," Joey said to Horace Burstell. "It makes for better news than the visit, and I 'preciate it a good ton. You can come here anytime you ain't broken through on your way out."

Joey thought their joint laughter would scare off any forest or mountain animal or harbinger, bringing up that odd word back from a school teacher he once met on his only train ride ever.

It all made him think he better make a back door in the cabin so he could escape into the cave if he had to, feeling positive that there was an exit back there he plain hadn't got to yet, like Horace hadn't found was way out yet.

With due application and a woodsman's tenacity, he constructed the new entrance/exit way with a clear route to the mouth of the cave to wherever it went, north, south, east or west, up-country or down country, up-river or down, any place where a single flake of gold said, 'Whoa, horse, this here's the place for us.'

And so, came the day for Joey Charlo when he heard, from a short way he thought from the cabin, the mighty roar of a big Black Bear sounding like he was proclaiming long-held ownership to the cave or the cabin or the whole of Flake Mountain, him being big enough to make such a claim. The outer parts of the cabin shook with the roars, as if it was going to collapse right there around him and him locked into its rubble.

As he slipped out the back door of the cabin, Joey said, "Horace, I hope I have better luck that you've had so far. This here critter sounds like he means business and I'm bound for elsewhere. I hope you hear him too and can somehow make way on your own."

Joey took a small tool sack with him and, of course, his big blunderbuss, half the size of his cabin door.

He was at the mouth of the cave when the loudest roar ever came and he saw his old cabin shake like it had never shaken in the worst of storms. A chunk of one side fell away by its whole self and smashed into pieces on other rubble, and with a terrible rumble the roof fell down in one solid piece until that too was smashed apart with a chilling sound of destruction.

And a huge Black Bear, near as big as a hunk of Flake Mountain, stood roaring at his devastation, as though it was a chunk of good old Justice itself.

At the mouth of the cave, looking back at the bear and his flattened wreckage spread twice as wide as the cabin had been, Joey Charlo dropped his tool kit, loaded his old blunderbuss and took aim at the Big Black Bear roaring with a continuous ferocity as it looked at him, Joey thinking it was eye to eye, and about to come to take over what once might have been his old home at Flake Mountain.

Joey had a dozen thoughts race through his mind: "Sorry, Big Boy, but I didn't think anybody lived here: Never saw one sign of habitation here, Big Boy. I don't know where this place goes to, Big Boy, but it has to go someplace."

The old weapon was loaded, aimed, about to claim its latest victim to some extent, when Joey Charlo lowered the weapon, then dropped it, and ran deep into the cave, not listening to hear if the bear was chasing him, but yelling out, "Horace, I hope to Hell I have better luck than you."

He ran as fast as he'd ever run, hearing the roars of the bear get fainter behind him, until he spotted ahead of him a sudden patch of sunlight, and right there on the side of a new trail, complacent, a bit wearied, sat Horace Burstell, who said, "Glad to see you, Joey, been waitin' on ya seems a week or more."

The Small War of Kurt Knobson

Some of the other wranglers said Kurt was the most *literative* of them all, and quite a few of them had no idea of what the word meant, but it stuck on him and began to earn a few side saddle additions, like *smart ass on a pony*, and *the big word spiller or spitter,* all the other so-called approaches or reflections not mounting to a heap of spoiled beans.

Another wrangler might yell out *word cusser* or *voluptuous* after he learned the new word in the last saloon he'd been in, or thought he carried away a word or name to stick on Kurt, "after all, he ain't such a bad guy." Favorites, in a way, always enjoy special placements.

Talk went on like that in the Trip's End Saloon in the West Texas town of Broken Horn, a saloon like all others across the territory where fiction became truth, and truth became closer to the Good Book than any of the talkers dared to avow.

What none of them said or challenged was the fact that Kurt Knobson, their very own Kurt Knobson, was, without a doubt, the best damned shooter they'd ever seen using a pistol, like "He can't shoot a rifle off'n a rock pile but don't chance him with a pistol." It was classic testimony of a man who was deadly with one kind of weapon and close to getting killed if he used anything else beside his six guns steady on his hips.

It was a business approach from the giddyap; for none of them would ever chance a pistol-drawing contest with him. Life certainly had better bargains hanging around for the picking.

That was so until Roscoe Portel and his pistol-drawing claims came to town. He was an out-and-out braggart of the first order from the very first words he said; "This here's a new town and the minute I come here, I'm already the fastest gun in town, bar none and bet your last measly dollar on that." With that said, he quick-drew his pistols, both of them, and put a dot above the "i" and a dot in the center of both "o's" in the sign hanging above the entrance to the Trip's End Saloon.

It was the kind of big-mouthing and great shooting that few of them had ever seen, if any of them ever did.

One voice, only half an hour later, from the far corner of the saloon's front deck, in the middle of continuing loud-mouth bombast by the new arrival, managed to say. "You ain't none faster than our own fast-draw, Kurt Knobson. Nobody here ever challenged him to a draw, knowed he would be dead hisself before his gun cleared leather. How's that fit you for sizin'?"

"Don't bother me none," Portel said as he whipped one pistol up at his hip and had it aimed right at the speaker. "You tellin' me he's faster than that, with that sign lookin' like it does now? Speak up, mister, we're all waitin' for you to say whose side you're really on. That is, if you're plain willin' to keep shootin' off your mouth and not your gun hangin' like a dead turkey at your side. Is that what you're really carryin' for a sidearm, a dead turkey? Well, I'll be a son of a gun, if I do say so myself."

He paused again, staring from eye to eye, running the course of the crowd, and added, "There's a whole lot of meanin' in what I just said. A whole lot. Better swaller it now, every one of you. It's me givin' you fair warnin'."

In the stillness of the air that followed, his words hung like a piece of an echo left over from an old argument between two best friends about something nobody can remember, including the two gents doing the arguing. It was serious quiet, and there were no takers speaking up to be found among the quick dead.

Kurt, heading into town, saw the gathering outside the saloon and realized that mighty important work must be taking place. He slowed his mount to a mere walk, slipped off to one side and came into Broken Horn right behind the town stable and tied up his horse.

It was a safe-rather-than-sorry move because he had not seen such a crowd gathered in all his years outside the saloon instead of inside. Somehow, he felt a drama mounting; if he could squeeze it, it would yell.

He observed the crowd begin its saunter for suds in a regular file of quiet folks into the saloon, a sign that a kind of control had been employed and thirst was in the order. He waited until the crowd was all inside the saloon and then approached the building from the alley between structures.

At the edge of the door, peeking in cautiously, he heard but one voice above the din. "Nobody but me is best gunman here in this town. I keep sayin' it and you keep makin' faces at me and I sure don't take too good to that kind of treatment. Hero's is larger than life and I'm larger than that, no matter what you think or so in your little minds."

In that manner, Portel carried on, a blistery, mind-blowin' attack on anyone and anything that dared stand up to him.

Kurt, in the wings of things as it were, unseen and unheard from as yet, began to fully realize a few things; that this town, by an accident, had been his town in a non-blustery and acceptable way since he had fired his first few rounds with unerring accuracy, had been top gun.

Kurt held a quiet, non-blasphemous grip right from the beginning. There was no embellishment to his simple accident of being so good with a gun that it was never questioned.

That made him feel good, and a sudden side-thought made him think about the responsibilities that went wearing some unseen type of crown, a King of the Hill situation and one loaded with growing pains in the face of the newest blowhard.

There was something to be done before things really got out of hand. All the known faces flew through his mind and not a one found pause to consider him to be the savior type. Not the heartiest one in the crowd and not the least, secretive, shyest of the lot, Mopy Derdock, who was born with tears in his eyes, both eyes "liquidated," to use the phrase in another manner.

Kurt ran the gamut of every one of his acquaintances, and not one measured up but himself. It was his call. His decision. His doing to get done.

"Might as well get it done and start now," he said with a most noticeable calm as he stepped forward and entered the Trip's End Saloon in his home town of Broken Horn, Texas.

Silence, a ringing, unparalleled silence suddenly gripped the saloon, as each and every customer, including the big mouth now about town, twisted around to see Kurt Knobson come the way some of them had dreamed up front, a ringing challenge to the newcomer.

"Why don't you shut your fat mouth, Mister, and put your guns into action instead of your fat tongue I swear's goin' to swaller you whole someday."

Every breath in the room was abated, drawn back from its moving out-ward, and put back to rest in each chest.

Portel swung about, itchy hands stiff in the air at each side, as if he was going to shoot the young speaker standing in the doorway looking like a half-grown boy, his gray sombrero tipped back at a new angle for him. It sat there in a kind of a cocky re-introduction to many old friends and the new man in town now frozen in place, who was hearing the first words of defiance from the entire town of Broken Horn.

The youngster in the doorway continued his challenge; "Since you got nothin' to say, fat-mouth, let's go outside and let these guns of ours do the talkin' for each one of us and for the whole town of Broken Horn, and," at which point he hesitated before adding, "for the first and last time." The steel in the boy's voice almost rang in the room like a steam train whistle hustling down the track.

Then Kurt Knobson gave out some general directions. "We, me and you go out first and then the others can follow behind us and get into some good places for cover in case we let any stray or wild shots get away from us."

"So, what do we do, plow boy? Stand around and twiddle our fingers?" Portel's manner, including his voice range, had changed, coming back to his near-natural grunt-and-groan delivery. But there were subtle changes in his whole person that a keen observer might notice, how a stiffness seemed to set onto his legs as if he'd never be able to mount a horse a do a jig with any ladies of the rooms above. Above all of that, his shoulders appeared thinner, weaker, than earlier bombastic moments.

If he knew he was being measured, he'd change in a second, but he was totally absorbed with the young man standing in the middle of the road, and pointing him out to a similar place, about 50 paces away in the middle of the dusty road through the center of Broken Horn.

Heaven, Earth, and Hell sat right down between them, no grips, no horns, no reins to hold onto.

In the midst of a tenacious crowd pulling for one favorite, the two-armed men, facing each other, were alone.

No more words were spoken.

In the flicker of a single eyelash, a second flicker took place, two shots were fired, and two men lay dead in the dusty road of Broken Horn, one once fully out-spoken, and one plainly and solemnly duty-bound. Age made no difference between them.

Being a Cowtown Santa for a Time

Christmas was coming. Who'd be Santa Claus had suddenly gotten sticky.

There had to be forty or so kids living in the town, all of them in squashed-in rooms in a dozen buildings, the pigeons on the roof often mingling with the kids at tall hide-'n'-seek, romances in dark budding, now and then some contraband or stolen goods getting exposed, two or three gymnasts every generation that managed and used the roof tops for exercises, dares, escapes of one sort or another. Merton Place, from various points of view, was a western city in itself.

And Christmas was coming. It was around the corner.

And Tony Andrelli and Studs Noffclip had been here longest of the tenants and enjoyed liberties that others had not attained. Tony collected the rents for the owner who was never seen in town, and Studs was responsible for light maintenance ... for that's all there was outside of the self-taught, self-fixers in this inner population for whatever goods or trade could get them. The favors for such work extended in all directions, north, south, east, west and up and down ... the up and down usually was a mutual sharing of tenderness and decent excitement under good cover or locked doors.

And Christmas was coming.

The two hirelings received free rent for their labors, each task differing by varying degrees depending on natural damages (like lightning, rust, leaky roofs, lay-offs, ... the general store where credit was tempted, hampered, shunned, punished), intentional complexities forcing or demanding Studs Noffclip's intervention with a night visit, tenant characteristics like smoldering anger and jealousy of a father whose weekly pay on his own job often did not cover the full rent or only a heavy portion of it, an amazingly slow, teasing handover of rent accompanied by unsaid promises from an older daughter of a young widow, for Death and Banishment, both being kind of an exile, hung in the late shadows as though they had also rented space on Merton Place.

Tony was a good-looking forty-year old widower of a dozen years who viewed Merton Place as a kind of heaven, swearing he'd never leave there. Studs Noffclip was fifty if a day, had a better sense of humor than Tony, could be lied to by adults and kids alike because none of the lies were allowed to mean anything to him or his relations with people. He swaggered home late on Saturday evenings now and then when he'd "leave the territory" so his footprints, fingerprints, bloodline and owed favors had no traceability. He could carpenter an unlevel door, fix a leak as if he'd said "See Studs in reverse," repair a break with the best of them and could wallpaper a room or a hallway (at one level) in one day ... for hire. He was called Mr. Fix-It by the ladies of the *town*.

His face was "Healthy-square," as one tenant fixed it, "like one of the heroes in the wall-drawn comics. You know, he'll be there when you need him, 'no doubt about it, no bout adout it.' He'd stick his finger in a grinder to save your kid or mine. He's not as good looking as Tony, but he's warmer, his curls are still in place on the back of his neck and sexy where his T-shirt shows him off, and if he ever lets go of that smile of his he'd own more places than the landlord. But it's got to be reserved for someone special and it looks like she ain't here yet."

That view found agreement all over Merton Place, from the ladies, daughters, boys whose rigs and saddles needed fixing and helpless fathers who looked at odd jobss like they'd look upon a thick, leather-bound book of Western Civilization.

To a woman they called Tony "Lover-Boy," some of them directly in person, and with or without smiles or any serious leaning to their intent ... as so read by the general population of Merton Place ... with curiosity. Tony, on the other hand from Studs' stand, was suspicious of every story told him by renters, by their daughters and sons if substituted at due day. He felt they impacted his standing in the community, made him a lesser man than was his fellow worker.

"Being lied to cheapens both sides of a story." Tony's heaven should not be rocked by such insults, as they twisted his view of mankind. All duties and directions should be easy and comfortable; a "yes," "no," or "I sure will as soon as I'm done with this one," did the trick.

On rent day they called him, "Grouchy, a sour man without glasses or moustache."

Mrs. Heckles (her real name FYI) yelled out her window to Tony Andrelli, caught down below as a light snow whipped between her building and the next one, 12 feet apart, where the widow Dunne lived on the low level with her brood of kids, all six with her blood, from ages four to 15, and her husband dead for six of those years, rental funds now in return for good graces, Mrs. Heckles might advise. She knew that Marcy Dunne would hear every word and actively join the conversation, as Tony Andrelli particularly favored one of the Dunne boys.

"Hey, Tony, if you want a hot coffee, c'mon over. Christmas is comin' and I'm markin' the way. If you don't like my brand of coffee on a cold day just before Christmas is comin', I'm sure Marcy across the way has another kind you'll probably like."

The window was wide open and a few flakes and a slight breeze came in as company, only making her shiver a little bit so long as she could deliver her message. "Hey, what the heck," she continued,

"Christmas is comin'," remembering one time she had thrown a bit of light garbage out the window into the tight alley and Tony saw her do it and never told Studs Noffclip. It would mean something to Studs but not to Tony. "People did such things," he'd probably muttered to himself, and then lied about it or evaded it entirely. You had to take three steps to their one to keep ahead of them, lies covering more ground than one can imagine, even on a snowy, cold day and Christmas on the horizon.

Marcy Dunne's window snapped open and she leaned out into the soft snow. "Tony," she yelled in a voice softened from usual, "I heard you were going to be Santa Claus this year for the little kids. I'm glad to hear that. You'll make a great Santa Claus for them and for us too, us old but not too old folks. Bring me a present when you get a chance." She didn't wait for an answer, didn't look at Deborah Heckles, and shut the window with loud punctuation.

The snow continued in the alley, the sky getting grayer and grayer, the flakes smaller and smaller. Old timers knew the difference.

Tony said to Studs, window to window of their separate buildings, "Some one of them's elected me as Santa Claus this year, and I hate that stuff. They'll try to fill me with a bunch of lies and bologna about the rent and I hate that stuff. I really hate it. They lie with their back teeth floating on their tongues like the Devil's rotating the liar's tiller by hand. You have to do me a favor, Studs. You got to be Santa Claus. I can't handle that stuff. It drives me crazy. They lie like tomorrow's never coming down the home stretch."

"Think they'd get mad? Any of them?" Studs spoke seemingly just above a whisper as if night was bringing guests, or he didn't want the topic to transfer to all the tenants. The evening, though, came descending in spasms of shades caused by the snow and a sudden brisk breeze, and night was in the spasms flickering with the snow and the town window's lights and a fireplace's red and yellow leaking a yellow glow clawing its way between houses, from where they burned nightly in the tight curves of Merton Place, oftentimes the signal to "the way home."

Studs realized, for the first time, as he leaned at the window, that he was bigger and stouter than Tony, especially around the gut, and would make a better-looking Santa Claus than Tony. Whoever played the part would never measure up to Jackson, who had a gift for it, who didn't have to pick up a red and white outfit once a year to improve himself. Jackson was different than all of them ... him, Tony, the landlord, the tenants. He wondered if the red and white suit had transformed him from what he might have been.

It all made him think heavily.

Studs was looking out his back window at the rest of the town, now shrouded by the thin whitish-grayish curtain of snow, so light it promised a heavy and constant fall. They were in for a good one. A swift thought slammed into him ... an army buddy swallowed by an avalanche on a trip high in far western mountains, the only time they had ever climbed that high, he and his old comrades. They hunted two days and never found him, never went back, that band of comrades, never together again.

"All the ladies are counting on you, Tony, so that means their kids. That's the way it stands. Too bad old Jackson had to pass on. He was a great Santa for a dozen years. I thought he'd never leave us, the kids really loved him, even the ones that have grown up and pass Christmas like it doesn't count anymore. That Junkins kid's a perfect example. Never learned a thing from Christmas, never gave anything to anybody except heartache to his folks and ten straight facing him in jail for one stupid mistake."

"You believe that, Studs, that it was a mistake? Kid's been a liar his whole life. I saw it way back. He even stole from Jackson one time, nothing big, but stole a package."

The falling snow drew Studs out of the past and he wondered what Tony really thought about when things happened to kids, like Spud Junkins. Tony had told him, on the sly, that he had seen Junkins steal a package from Jackson's door. "Took it like it was his own. Stuffed it in his shirt like he used to load up on candy at the general store."

"You tell Jackson? You never told Arthur any of that stuff."

Somehow, with all past histories of the "known felons in our midst," as Tony whispered, chanted, dispensed as a guarded aside even when they were away from their own *cul-de-sac*, Studs didn't have to imagine what Tony was thinking, or in this case, cross over to the next building to find out.

He looked at Tony as Tony studied the snow, determining that he too saw the snow as small pieces of a blanket that would cover everything in sight. Eventually, it would hide all surfaces, all projections, all outlines, under its cape, coat, canvas, coverlet, whatever they'd call it. For starters, the finest snow falling for hours was able to hide monuments, the four presidents of the mountainous park, the highest peaks of the Rockies, the Alps, the Himalayas, the Pyrenees, all the mountains he'd try to forget himself, that even Jackson had tried to forget in his imaginative cruises through Hell, as well as all the lies and feeble excuses ever told. Perpetration, at least, buried for a season.

Was Christmas any different there, in those other places we never been?

The split in the two-way conversation and attendant thoughts came with a sudden and strident female voice from outside. "Tony, if you were thinking of wearing Jackson's Santa Claus suit, you're not getting the chance. Myrtle just told me it went out with the trash one day. She says she doesn't know who tossed it, but it's gone, been gone since just after the funeral, July not having much call for Santa Claus get-ups."

There was a pause. "You better hurry down to the general store to try to get another one. He's going to close down pretty soon. If you don't get it there, you'll have to go to Cotton City in this weather to get one."

Tony, Studs knew, hadn't been in Overton's General Store since the great argument over ten years ago. He wouldn't go now. And he'd never get to Cotton City in this snow, the wind now whirling, the breeze gone to a wind, the spasms now crossed over from sorry palpitations to aches and pains and pure anguish for anyone on the trail ... and Christmas Eve not holding back for anybody or anything, even old Jolly Nick with a grouch as rough as sandpaper. That's what the successor-by-demand for Santa Claus had looked like since he had assented to motherly demands. "Motherly" meaning one mother in particular and no name crossing Studs' lips.

"I can't do it, Studs. I know I promised, but I can't do it. No Overton's either. Never that."

Tony was looking at Studs as if a favor was due, not eye-to-eye, but keeping his head lowered like one lion in a cage of two, his brows just touching the soulful pupils to be seen where they sat in the fluid of sympathy's request.

Studs was measuring his silent neighbor, the speed of the wind now accompanied by screams, screeches, howls coming off building corners, edges of roofs where ice tended to build up in the old days. Studs didn't look at his wrist watch or the wall clock behind him. He studied more of the lights out beyond them. Saw a dozen more distant lights in a matter of seconds dim, twinkle, sputter, die out. Sideways in a hurry came the snow, banks of it, clouds of it, billowing white, blinding. Travel was out for the night; it was Overton's or no Santa Claus for the kids, and for the herd of mothers.

Studs got to Overton's just as the lock clicked in the door, Harry on his way home. He opened the door for Studs, greeted him like an old friend. "What brings you down here, Studs?"

"I need a Santa Claus suit. Jackson's was thrown out by accident."

"I got just what you need, yes sir, just what you need. Perfect fit. Tried it on another fellow just yesterday and he thought he was swimming in the Red Sea. Imagine that." His smile was as wide as a canyon.

"Don't I have to try it on?"

"No worries, Studs, a perfect fit, I swear. Like that jacket I saved for you. A perfect fit, and at a reduced price." He looked closely at his watch. "Melva will shoot me if I'm late. She worries about my riding since that last accident, her sanity, she says."

His hands were wrung as if he were squeezing pain from them. "Look," he said quickly, as he checked the time again, "one dollar for the holiday, two dollars for keeps. No buy around like this one." He sent one of his special Overton looks; it said all he could amass (Melva waiting, the snow relentless, the traffic forbidden, past favors all lined up in a row.)

"I'll take it for the $2.00," Studs said triumphantly, just the way Overton liked it, he was sure.

Tony's light swung twice and Studs opened his window. "You get it?" Tony said.

"Yup, I got it. Christmas Eve tomorrow and we're all set."

"You're a real pal, Studs," Tony said and brought his window down with a quick slam. Snow, the light fluffy kind, flew off the window sill, and running drops of melted snow showed on the window as it hit the sill. Studs couldn't see Tony turn away from the window, but he knew he did, as usual when he was through window talking.

Christmas Eve rolled in on top of a day's shoveling, shovels at work all parts of the day, the alleys cleared, horses all barned, kids throwing snowballs, Studs in a relentless attempt to get into the Santa Claus suit that was generations too small for him. No part of it was sufficient for him.

Time pushed its way forward.

The younger kids were down in the snow, dancing in the curve of the road, in the great act of waiting on Santa Claus, the secret pile of gifts locked in Sadie Quinn's closet, the key in Studs' pocket.

Studs Noffclip figured it was time; it didn't come as retribution, but as a piece of reality that had been bent out of shape, that needed fixing.

He swung the light, his signal to Tony.

Tony's light replied and he pushed up his window and leaned out. "What is it, Studs? You ready?"

Studs let it go. "It doesn't fit me, Tony. I can't get one piece on. Not one arm or one leg. It's too damned small. It's your size. It's a special fit for you."

Tony had never said it before, not this way. "You're lying to me, Studs. That's your problem. You promised." It looked as if he was going to slam his window down on top of Christmas Eve. That would be the end of it all, he was certain. Everything they had ever done, alone or together, as a team, or as agents for the landlord.

But there was left-handed support in the matter for Studs as he thought about settling with Overton, but more so, saving Christmas Eve for the toddlers, the kids, the ones hanging on the edge of Santa Claus, their fingers in the final grip, mothers with their fingers crossed for one more year of innocent smiles, acute acceptance.

Mild, sometimes passive, always pleasant, well-liked though he was getting stouter than ever, "He'll never be as lean as Lover-Boy," Studs Noffclip leaned way out the window and yelled, "Marcy Dunne, will you come up here to see me. It's pretty important." His voice shot down into the alley like a bomb had exploded.

A single light swung an arc in Tony Andrelli's place; he was *wearing* his old black jacket, soon it would be a red jacket, of that Studs was sure ... he knew Tony as well as anybody ever would, both sides of him, the outer and the inner. The only thing he'd worry about would be the Santa Claus smile, the "Merry Christmas" salutations, how Tony might handle his own biggest lies.

Time and snow tide would tell.

Ransom Doak, Shooter Extraordinaire

From the day, the very first day, when a pistol came into his hand, from his mother, of all people, young Ransom Doak knew the edge, beauty, and balance of its comfort. He was six-years old handling his first gun, his mother approaching 40 years, and her husband dead at the hands of a marauder looking for a cheap and quick meal from the lady in a log cabin only an echo outside the small town of Small Parallels, Texas.

His first shot at a bucket big enough to catch a shotgun blast, didn't move the bucket, but killed his pet rabbit, which his mother eventually cooked for supper.

"No, Ransom, darling, you hurried that shot too much. Remember, always remember, the target belongs to you." She knew she had to make the point of all this stick in the boy's mind for a lifetime, so she made the words hard and true, and as solid as night's surety; black as forever, solid black, a deed calling for the death of a murderer.

"You own it from now until the skies fall down on us, and believe me, dear boy, they will fall down again someday, like they did when your father was shot in the back at his work. His killer, from that day until forever comes, belongs to us. The passage has been made. The Good Lord provides for that. You keep that face of his in your mind for all your life until that rotten killer finds the bullet that owes him is already lodged in his chest, the one put there by me or by you, and I prefer that you do it. Claim it back for yourself, my darling boy, now load up that pistol, practice when you can and I will sell my soul to get money for us and for a new pistol set for you for your 12th birthday, when that day comes.".

Ransom Doak shot his pistol for hours in a day, every day, as he watched the men come from town to visit his mother, and the jar of money in her secret place in the barn grew by pounds and mounds.

Well before he was 12, the pistol was a delicate instrument in his hand, to his eye, as his targets became smaller, the aims better, the notoriety of "the kid shot" moving around the territory beyond Small Parallels, far and wide as some folks told it, including the story behind the story, and many men wanted to be in on the coming kill.

But none of them ever had that killer's face locked into their minds as Ransom and Edna Doak did. He was broad across the forehead, almost cliff-like in its shape, thick at the chin and lips, nose might have been winged by a stray shot much earlier in life, a capital mark for any man to carry about in his life, including not going near Small Parallels for years on end. Both ears were pinned back as if he was listening to two sides of everything, here and there, hither and yon, up and down, out front and in back, and both ends of the local canyon as well.

They were talking one day at the woodpile as Ransom was doing his day's work at the pile of split logs, swinging the ax like a 100-pound sword as it came down in the top face of a log to split it like a slash from King Arthur on his horse, the power like a strike from a God on high, a god of the saddle.

"My boy," she said, visibly impressed with his strength and dexterity, "you master many things in your days. What you touch, you own. What you do, becomes you. Remember the face that only we two know in all of Texas. I have the strange feeling that destiny comes near for us, for your father, for the man with the killer's face. I think he is near. After all these years, he has dared to return. Though I have not seen him, I feel him to be near. We must be ready for the moment."

She gathered a few things, placed them in her carriage and said, "I will go into town and look around. If he is here, I will let you know. That is my promise to you."

She was about to start off when Ransom swung the ax like a gunshot and another log split into two pieces. "You are so good at that, Ransom. Keep working and we'll have winter's pile ahead of schedule."

"I'll do that, Mother, and straighten up the pile while I'm at it. Have a good day." He returned to his chore as she headed into Small Parallels.

When she was out of sight, he felt the strangest of feelings rush up and down his frame, up and down his arms and legs, leaving a kind of message in his whole body that Time was touching him in a brand-new way, one not ever felt before, not ever known before. But it was acceptable to his whole body, as if questions and answers were in orbit in and about him. In a series of motions, mind pictures, quick images striking with a powerful force, he was armed, and began saddling his horse.

A once-known feeling of death and desperation was racing through him, and he felt like he had been warned by notice and armed to the hilt.

His horse, a highly-favored black stallion named Black T, Ransom's horse for nearly ten years, raced a route different from Ransom's mother's path. Ransom judged that they'd be in Small Parallels before her, figure out what was pulling at both of them, for surely some single sway had moved each of them to be on alert, to be wary for each other. It would be havoc to let some hideous villain have the upper hand, the first hand, the loaded gun in hand before its victim knew it was raised against him or her.

Life, as it had been known, could come crushing down upon them in spite of old hates and atrocities, in spite of outright murder old as the ages, and at the hands of the killer from years-past.

As he passed by a tie rail, one black stallion, a beauty of a horse, neighed a recognition to him, as if saying hello after a long separation. There was no doubt it was his father's horse, Black Messenger, stolen by his father's killer years ago, still healthy, still black as coal dust, as black as night itself.

They had a quick reunion and Ransom whispered, "You'll be going back home with us tonight, Blackie, I promise you that. No long-time murderer riding on your back all over the country. Not anymore. Now, I'm going to see what's what in the saloon and who's who, bet your bottom dollar on that, Blackie, your whole bottom dollar."

Kid gunsmith Ransom Doak slipped into the saloon, quickly scanned the room, saw mostly known faces or new faces of no interest to him. Yet one man, faced away from him, carried a thickness of hair showing under his sombrero and laying on the board of his thick neck.

A certainty began to fill Ransom Doak, as to who the man was, not a local he could tell immediately, but a newcomer for sure. Ransom felt the grinding in his stomach in his whole chest as he blurted words he had saved for years, "Hey, skunk killer, with the face I haven't seen in many years, but I was tipped off because my father's horse is looped to the rail out front, the horse taken by my father's low-down skunky killer who has run right into my gun range where I been waiting all these years."

There was an elongated silence, the big man didn't move for long seconds, some folks thinking Ransom Doak, with only a view from the man's backside, might have made a mistake.

The silence, the intakes of breath, filled the room, and the big man said, "Whoever you are, I came to town on the stage, Go find the stage driver and ask him."

"No, you didn't," said an unknown voice across the room, "I saw you alight from the saddle of a big black right out front only a few hours ago. He turned to Ransom Doak and said, "Honest, Ransom. I wouldn't kid you on that. Right off a big black he leaped like he was going to own the place. Made me look at him a couple of times. He's the dude, I swear on the Good Book."

Reality often comes in different sizes and in a variety of announcements, and when they are attested to by a sideways leap of a cornered man and a drop to his knees on the floor, his gun in his hand, the bullet meant for vengeance and carried for years was in his heart before he could pull his own trigger. Vengeance was quicker than protection.

The widow Doak heard the single gunshot and thought she best check on the excitement. Ransom surely was back at home, but she could never tell about that boy except she believed he had moves she'd never seen.

A Freighter's Connection

Creighton Glastenbury, last of his family, impoverished from birth despite his name and lucky to get to his 16th birthday, found his journey working on a wagon train ending in the small California town of Newbridge. Across seven state borders he had traveled seeking warm weather, safe winters, and a chance to find a cause other than simple survival. He was tired of the eternal scratching for meals, good cover over his head, and silence in the night. The stars of evening, holding sway like magnificent emeralds over wide grass, were his greatest comfort, took him to sleep most nights of the journey though he shared them with coyotes, owls and other creatures of impending darkness. He remembered at odd hours an old Indian, met out on the trail, saying, "Count on the stars. They do not fail." When one of the stars, loose as a runaway horse, streaked across the pebble-lit sky, he found comfort in it, and once in a while a sign of coming luck.

"Listen, Crate," the wagon master had said as he just about turned his own wagon around to start back to the beginning of places, "stay with me and earn good keep and you'll find a place for yourself. It's in the cards for you. You've earned some kind of a good deal coming to you." He had enjoyed the young man's company along the long trail, saw how he applied himself in harsh situations, had a head for fixing broken wagon parts, and could follow orders to the letter. Skill with a gun hand was also part of his make-up.

"I'll stay here, Mr. Robichaud. I got a name from a fellow back in Missouri, said to look him up, make a stab at staying. He runs a small freight outfit."

"What's that freighter's name, Crate?"

"'Willie Budroy,' said the Missouri man."

"Well, Crate, you're in luck. I know Willie Bud from way back in the territory. I'll give you a note to him. We rode a team awhile. Yes, sir, old Willie Bud. Damned good man, too."

The two parted company, and young Glastenbury, with a note in his pocket and a name on his tongue, went looking for a potential mutual friend. He rode his own horse and carried two pistols on his gunbelt. From his experience on the long trail, from his study of meeting people, he looked the part not of a young teenager, but a seasoned killer, a shooter. Learning to impress people was one lesson he carried off on the road across the country, from Pennsylvania to a spot beside the Pacific Ocean. He thought the place looked to be next to heaven, if that was at all possible.

"How can you explain it, son," the freighter Budroy said, "that an old pal of mine would write a note for you, but not look me up?" He nodded, smiled and said, clearly from a fond memory, "Robichaud a damned good man. I'd take his word afore anybody's."

"He said he was making one more trip and would settle here in Newbridge soon as any place else. Said he likes how the land sits between the mountains and the ocean."

"And a gent in Missouri gave my name to you? Who was that?"

"Name was Harold Clockson. I helped him out of a problem one time, out on the trail."

"What kind of trouble, son? You dig right in for him?" Budroy, holding his head at an inquisitive angle and his eyes right on Glastenbury's eyes as if an answer would be written there in a clear hand. "You do tend to cut things short of the end sometimes."

Glastenbury, admiring Budroy's direct way of speaking, said, "Well, sir, he was in a tight bit of trouble from two gents on the road and I rode right into the middle of it coming over a small hill. They had guns drawn on him and said they had no interest in me and I could pass on by."

"What did you do, son?"

"I said, quick like it would make a difference, 'This man's my father and I don't truck with anyone holding guns on him, not one but two of them, like you're afraid of him one on one. You ought to be. He's faster than me with that pistol of his, and I am damned good at it.'" One hand still held the reins, the other, like a loose weed in a soft breeze, hung near his holstered pistol.

"Yeh? And?" Budroy said, his face carrying an expectant look of glee, the smile about to break loose. After all, that brazen kid was right now in front of him and had obviously survived a scary situation.

"One of them robbers laughed and pointed at Mr. Clockson and then was going to point at me and I drew and shot the pistol right out of his hand. The other gent's horse almost tossed him out of the saddle and I had a gun right directly in his face in a second or two. We let both of them go, but I told them I was good at drawing and was going to give the sheriff a poster make-up on them so they better get out of the territory before they got hung as horse thieves on top of being roadside robbers to boot."

"Marvelous, son, marvelous. How'd you think about all that stuff so fast? Him being your father, the horse thief bit, the whole thing? Can you really draw good pictures?"

"One of them was riding a Circle-T brand and I know they didn't work for Circle-T. And I can't draw a straight line with a plumb board to guide me, not if it took me a whole day."

"Son, I'd want you riding on my rig any day of the week. You are now working for me. You got a place to stay?"

"Not yet."

"You have one now," Budroy said, his deep smile coming canyon-wide. "You can have my old shack. Needs a bit of work, but I'm sure you can do it up good." He pointed over his shoulder, behind his new barn. "That's it back there." The smile was wide again on his face.

"You'll really like my team of horses. They're Clydesdales, over 17 hands, both of them, and stronger than a herd of buffalo. Come all the way from Scotland, they did, like sailors crossing the whole dang ocean in one trip. We'll be going off tomorrow or the next day for another delivery. I got to advise you there's been some trailside activity hereabouts makes me glad you'll be riding with me."

"What kind of trailside stuff, Mr. Budroy?"

"They call you Crate, do they? Well, you can call me Willie from now on, Crate. And I heard a couple of stages got robbed and a freighter was relieved of some of his goods just more than a week ago. I'll be a little bit more comfortable with you sitting in the bucket seat with me."

Early on the morning of his second day in Newbridge, they were out a half dozen miles on the main trail, when Glastenbury saw at a distance two riders coming toward them. He studied their trail manners for a few minutes and said, "Willie, we got suspicious company up there ahead of us, and I'm going to get comfortable on the load, sort of out of sight."

He grabbed his rifle and slid up on top of two crates wrapped in canvas, squeezing himself down in between the two crates. The two riders he could see clearly from where he peeked between the canvas shrouds.

From his view, the young shotgun rider saw the two men with hands hanging too close to their side arms for neighborliness. And they looked nervous as they came closer, with the pair splitting up and moving to each side of the wagon, another knock on their neighborliness.

One of the men drew his gun and waved it at Budroy and said in a harsh and demanding voice, "Hold it there, old man. We aim to take something off your hands. Don't make any trouble and we'll let you go with most of your freight. We want just the one package going to the Three Circles Ranch. Now you hop down out of there and we'll all be quiet about this." He waved the gun again.

Glastenbury, fast as a hawk on the dip, put a single round into the hand carrying a pistol and had the rifle trained on the other man before he could move.

"Take your boots off and throw them up here along with your weapons." He waved the rifle at both of the robbers. They dismounted, took off their boots and threw boots and weapons up on the top of the wagon, seething all the while, curses and grunts coming loose from the bottoms of their souls. "We'll get you for this, kid," the wounded man said.

Glastenbury put a round into the ground near their horses and the two animals went off at a gallop and out of sight over a small hill. The hoof beats could be heard getting fainter and fainter until there was no more sound from them.

"If you go looking for your boots, I got a pretty good idea you'll know where they are, if you dare come that close. In the meantime, we're going to find your pal at Three Circles Ranch who gave you information about this load. That sure ain't going to sit well with those folks over there."

He put another round right between the two men, making them dive for cover, and then yelled, "Giddy up," to the wagon team, and the wagon rolled on its way.

"You think they'll come looking for them boots, Crate?" Budroy said.

"About once at the most," he replied, looking back over his shoulder at the men going gingerly after their horses, their tender feet making visible statements.

At the Three Circles Ranch, the freight master said to the ranch owner, "This here's my new hire. Name's Crate. He'll tell you what happened on the road here. Real interesting, if I do say so."

He paused and said, "Go ahead, Crate. This gent, Max Burnham, owns the spread. Tell him what you know."

Glastenbury, speaking a little louder than necessary, for more of an audience than just the owner, said, "Mr. Burnham, two gents, both husky sorts with battered gray Stetsons like they been trod on in a dirty road, wearing a gray shirt on one fellow and a checkered black and white shirt on the other, riding a gray and a paint both about 14 hands, knew all about the delivery coming to you. They said directly they wanted only one piece, the one we just unloaded for you. Said they would let us move on. So, we want to make sure you know that someone here, we think on your payroll, told them fellows all about it."

"That's quite a story, son. Any more to it?"

"Yep," Glastenbury said, "one of them's got a bad hand that I quick shot. He must still be hurting. If he ain't bound to get out of the territory about now, you might be able to find him." The hesitation in his voice said some other pertinent facts were coming. "The last I saw of them, on the road back there, they had no guns on their belts, no boots on their feet, and no horses under them."

"Oh, I know who they are, son. I want to welcome you to Newbridge. You've made a good start already." He smiled and looked at the house set back against some tall trees.

As they were leaving Three Circles, Budroy said, "Crate, you missed something back there you ought to be interested in. I guess you don't see everything." He leveled a hard stare at his young employee.

The new hire, smiling, said, "Oh, I saw her, Willie. Ain't she some kind of a beauty? Looks like a prairie flower all shining by itself on the grass. I saw her the minute we rode into the place, her checking me out from the window at first, then from the doorway, hiding but not hiding, if you know what I mean?"

"Crate," Budroy said, "I don't think I could catch up to you if they gave me another 50 years to do the job. The girl's name is Emily, Burnham's only kin. A horse killed her mother a few years ago. He sets all his store on her. She's your age." He realized he had learned a whole lot from his new hire in a short time and laughed almost all the way to their next delivery.

Putting the team away that night, he was still smiling at his good luck, and the luck of Creighton Glastenbury. He had no question about who made the best pairing of the day: his set of Clydesdales, true giants of the road; him and Crate, new pards of a sort in the freight business; or Crate and Emily Burnham, something beautiful about to blossom in Newbridge.

Glastenbury wasn't right on all accounts, though. The two road agents came calling in the dead of night. They were almost into the house when squawking guinea hens in the trees woke the young striker from a deep sleep in his little cabin behind the barn. He was up and armed in seconds and ran to the house where the two intruders were trying to force open the ranch house door.

He fired off one warning shot, which was ignored by the two men, and he was forced to drop both of them before Budroy was out of bed. It was revealed that Burnham's men had chased the two robbers off into the grass, and lost track of them in the night. The band of hunters heard the gunfire at Budroy's place and came to investigate. They found Budroy and his new hire standing over the two wounded road agents bleeding on the ground, Glastenbury's gun still smoking.

And putting all things together, the way he usually handled his business and all that went on about him, Creighton Glastenbury didn't waste much time before he went calling at the Three Circles Ranch.

Micah Topaz, Born Sheriff

Some men, whether you believe it or not, come bidden by fate to fill holes in the human condition. So it was with Micah Topaz, born in a wagon train heading to California. He never got much further on the family journey than the place of his birth, a small corner of Nevada with the mountains staring them in the face. When the dispute among the wagon train leaders erupted, and deep factions developed, Micah's family decided to stay pretty close to where they were at the time. The place was called Mattsville.

Micah's father Armand had seen the long look at the mountains in his wife Hazel's eyes.

"What do you stare at, Hazel, you seem so set on something out there?"

It was part of the reason for loving her from the outset back in Pennsylvania, her careful attention to surroundings, the practiced moves she invested in her efforts, her concern for things that should be beautiful and could be counted on. She might have said the same things about her kitchen, but held that argument in place; Armand might not understand the full point of it, yet it was enough to make her content.

"I look at it this way, Armand; none of us swim too well and the view on the other side can't be any prettier than this one, just the ocean making a difference, and that only as far as it goes. And if I was to be asked, I'd settle on this side without the long walk ahead of us." She looked off again, at the majestic peaks marking out a huge chunk of the land, at the same time grasping at the blue sky. "Just think of all that being all ours for the next fifty years or so, the good Lord willing us along that far."

The family settled down at the foot of Brass Mountain, in the little town of Mattsville on a very busy stage line, and Armand Topaz, with a good sense of things mechanical, started a small business of repairing small arms, side guns, and rifles. His shop grew in pieces at the side of a small cabin that, in time and with hard work at horses and cattle filling his daylight hours, grew as the family grew.

Micah, as the first born, leaped quickly at all new interests, ready to take his place in the order of things. He rode, he hustled, he sweated; and he learned about horses, cattle, guns, taut leather and loose leather, strung wire and loose wire, the good and the bad that things might come one's way in the course of a day, with people always in the mix.

His parents, with some caution, kept a good eye on the resolute youngster as he grew into his britches, as his father was often apt to say to company that came to visit the ranch. Armand Topaz was also fond of saying, "The boy marks his day well." He would let others' observations fill in the cracks. On the side, in a daily exercise, the elder Topaz provided his promising son much food for thought; "Who rises earliest gets the first post holes dug and the first line of wire hung in place. More than the cows'll know the difference." He might also say, "The horse with the bad nail comes second to the horse with no bad nails," or, "One handgun oiled early and often has a keen chance of winning any marker."

So receptive was the youngster that all who knew him began to measure his steps, watch his work. All Mattsville knew who the comer was.

Micah Topaz was fourteen when the first real indication came that he would eventually wear a badge with true authority, that he was born for the office. Fate, of course, and a bit of habit having its way, its sense of routine, had a part in it.

On a very early and still dark morning ride he found their fence had been cut and a small section of their herd had been driven off through the break. It'd be hours, he reasoned, before he could roust enough neighbors and town men to go after the rustlers, so he took off after them on his own. A few hours later he found a single line of wire across a small passage between the walls of a small canyon, one that he had been in before. At the other end was a narrow fissure where escape was possible, but slow. He tried to put himself in the rustlers' boots, thinking what would be their next move.

His decisions came quickly, as did the flush of false dawn. He cut the strand of wire and tied it back up with small rawhide strings. On three poles he managed the same action, assuring any pressure would break the wire loose. With a quick start he rode around the ridge and came in from the other side. Thick silence sat in the small camp where four men were sleeping. So was the night guard a hundred yards back toward the wired end, his head dropped on his chest and completely motionless. The silence wrapped the small canyon like a boxed present; not a bird sounded, the cattle stood still, no animals made overtures of any kind. His steps were quiet as he tried to move like a shadow moves, hardly noticeable.

Right up behind the cattle, Micah softly stepped, saw the apparent lead animal with a huge spread of horns and fired the first of five rounds right over his head. The lead steer bolted and the rest followed as they broke for the wired end of the canyon.

Micah fired again as the rustlers' horses, caught in the rush, also bolted. Micah fired at the camp sight, scattering the wakened men, and then he retreated through the narrow fissure, mounted his horse, and rode back the way he had come. Most of the herd, and two of the rustlers' horses, were in the hands of Micah's father and a ranch hand. They had come looking for Micah. One of the horses was identified and later that day, at Kirk's Saloon in Mattsville, 14-year old Micah Topaz slipped a gun against Harry Macomber's gut in front of sheriff Bill Knox and explained the situation. Macomber had just told Knox that some hombre had tried to bushwhack him early in the day and had wounded his horse, which had run off, not to be seen again.

Micah had jumped right into the middle of the discussion, unlike any usual 14-year older. "I got your horse outside, Harry, and he's not hurt either. You're a liar and a rustler and your horse is proof of it. You were sleeping at your camp when you should have been on guard. I saw you and that Mexican sombrero you're always wearing. Some men are looking for your pals looking for their horses. We'll get them too. They'll be in here, probably in short order, before the day is out. You better get it off your chest now, else it'll be harder on you later on." Macomber admitted his part in the affair but wouldn't give up any names.

"First thing we ought to do," Micah said, "is to see if any cowpokes come into town without their horses. Three or four of them went afoot when I stampeded the cows. And they'll be needing new mounts soon as you know. It won't pin anything on them who come without their ponies, but it'll put the eye of the law square on their backs."

In the next half dozen years Micah Topaz, with ingenuity, young imagination and a keen eye, matched wits and skills with a variety of owl hoots, rustlers and desperadoes of various degrees, all of them with an eye on Topaz holdings or valuables cached in Mattsville. With the growing reputation out and about the territory, a small legend continually approached maturity.

Bill Knox, just before he gave up the job and headed for California himself, told everybody that Micah Topaz had come fully prepared to be the new sheriff. "He was born for this job and you ought to take advantage of his good nature, the way I mean it." He nodded at Kirk the saloon owner and a few more of the town's merchants and a few of the big ranch owners, the ones holding much of the town's riches in their hands. They also could dictate the appointment of the sheriff.

Micah Topaz was 21 years old that very day, and some people said, for the longest while, that Bill Knox had waited for Micah Topaz to come of age, legally, that is, for the young man was there well ahead of himself.

Teddie Silverado's My Name

He stood dirty, dusty, powerful dry, after a long ride for a short drink, and exclaiming to a nosy bartender at the Wobbly Cow Saloon, "Sure, that's my name, Teddie Silverado because I like it and my mother liked it better than the stupid one my father gave me, which I long ago have put back to sleep somewhere along the line."

It all started because the bartender, Jake Tawnwhip, had said, "What the Hell did you say your name was, Kunju Gavoto? It weren't the way I been hearin' it all this time you been hangin' in here."

Teddie Silverado, forever from that point, was called as he said he was, "Teddie Silverado," because the gun came out of his holster and was aimed over the bar directly at the mouth of Jake Tawnwhip, who had mispronounced Silverado's new true name for the second or third time in the conversation over a short drink of hard-learning and quick-spouting of a renamed cowpoke with a gun in hand.

One day it might save his life, but he hadn't thought of that possibility.

That didn't give Teddie much time, or the bartender, because that's the night the bank was robbed and three strangers wandered into the saloon, one at a time, later on while the sheriff and a hastily-formed posse had ridden out of town on the start of a useless chase ... of nothing in particular.

The three strangers, as if meeting for the first time, gathered at the bar. "Hell," said one of them to a heavily-bearded man wearing two guns on his hips and red suspenders over his shoulders as if they caused discomfort and a considerable stretching and working of their placement, "I heard the barkeep call that there gent 'Teddie Silverado,' and that's nothin' more than a made-up name from a story-teller 'round the campfire. Hell, like I said, 'that ain't your real name, is it?'"

The gun came off Teddie's hip faster than heavy-beard-and-red-suspenders could imagine, as it was stuck right in his face quicker'n he could breathe. "I ain't sayin' but once more, Teddie Silverado's my name, and anybody not likin' it's got somethin' against my mother and I don't favor that too much, 'specially in a saloon of all places."

"You got to be kiddin' me, kid. Don't you 'member me workin' with your daddy. Kunju Gavoto's what we called him and I'd call him that right now if he was here, but he ain't about to come here from where he got put down on the border with ole Mexico. And you don't like the name your daddy give you? Every poke I ever knew wore the name his old daddy give him from since Mary called the little boy Jesus."

He put his hand out as if to ward off Teddie's gun until he heard the tinny click of the tiny hammer on the weapon. "Whoa, son, I was a friend of your daddy's way back in the day. We wuz pards, to say the least, on drives and other long rides from here to the big river, ain't no place we weren't been."

He paused for a few extra breaths and said, "Who's the sheriff around here? Why don't he step up in the middle of this to-do?" He looked around as if waiting for a sheriff to step into the middle of things.

The barkeep said, "His name is Chuck Turner but he ain't here now."

"Where's he hidin'?"

"Leading a posse lookin' for the gang what robbed the bank last night."

"What'd they get?" he said as he leaned way over the bar and looked down below the backside of the counter.

"It ain't back here and it weren't much but a bunch of South money ain't good for much at all anymore, like it never really was, like the real Government says. Not worth the pot to pee in. Nothin' to those tied-up bundles of Greybacks the likes of Jefferson Davis on a $50 or Calhoun and some other bozo on a $1000, and all of 'em like I said, 'Not worth a pot to pee in."

"What the Hell's he chasin' after nothin' worth nothin'?" Looks more like it ain't even a crime, if nothin' was stolen. What's he in a stir about?"

The room full of men at sudden argument was still, the silence as if demanding responses of some nature, waiting for reason or fact to click into place.

Teddie Silverado, with his gun still in hand, stepping back into the conversation, said, "You ask some real stupid questions the more you talk, mister, like asking me about my name and all about the bank like nothing ever happened after all this mouthful of gopher crap. What the Hell are you really interested in?"

He swung his gaze about the room and clicked the hammer again, the sound running around the silent saloon, everybody in the room weighing in on the argument about value of nothing or nothing of value hanging right there in the middle of them like a schoolmarm might do it.

At that moment, the sun showing over the top of the saloon door, back from its latest trip elsewhere, the door popped open and a man with a badge on his chest marched right up to the bar, with six, dusty, dirty, powerfully dry men following him, his voice heavy as a pick ax, just as steady, just as demanding, said to the barkeep, "Jake, give 'em two, three drinks apiece on my tab, and not anymore on me and I know they got some settling-in to do on their own time and not mine. We run into exactly nothing out there like we was out on a date with the Widow Smithwick. Two-three drinks on me and nothing more on my account. Got me?"

As he finished his introduction to the whole saloon, he spotted Teddie Silverado, gun in hand, still levelled at heavy-beard-and-red-suspenders, and said, offhandedly, as if his shift for the day was done, "What the Hell are you two up to when we need our drinks more pronto that what you're at, that's for sure the way it looks to me," the other silence still in place, though his echo still had some body in it.

Heavy-beard-and-red-suspenders said, sort of hospitably, "Oh, Sheriff, I just heard you had the posse out there after criminals that didn't do no crime but rob the bank of nothin' at all worth anything at all; like it don't count at all, not from where I'm standin', me bein' Checker Wilson and this here gent aholdin' his pistol on me is Teddie Silverado from these here parts."

The man with the badge coughed a ludicrous cough.

"Was he going to shoot you, Checker Wilson, in front of all these people, and not a gun in your own hand, like you was already out-drawed in a Hell of a hurry? Don't tell me you were going to be killed by a gent with that kind of a name."

He coughed and laughed again and said, "Teddie Silverado like it's really Kunju Gavoto whose father rode with me on a few long jaunts near the end of the war before things turned heels overhead, if you know what I might mean."

To illustrate his point, he snapped the badge on his chest as though a statement of fact had been made, swallowed his second drink, snapped the glass back to the barkeep, "Nother, Jake, and just as smooth, before I have to take care of this argument about to happen, or an accident bigger than all of us and someone gets hung on the tree down the road a piece before any of us knows what really happened right in front of us."

"Naw," said Checker Wilson, "he weren't goin' to shoot me, Sheriff. I don't think the boy's got enough guts to pull the trigger right now," and he swung around as if he was about to draw his own weapon, at which the sheriff said, "Wilson, where'd you ever come from, and when, to be here when our bank was robbed of sacks and sacks of money?"

"Well," Wilson came back with, "up-country a ways, all the way to Canadi's border, a furer piece you can't go. And I don't think this misnamed boy of sorts was goin' to shoot me, not a chance in Hell of it."

He laughed a laugh of ridicule, fawned fear for the entire audience of the full saloon, stuck out his chest like he was king of all the trails in all of Texas, bar none.

Sheriff Chuck Turner jumped into the middle of things, snapping his glass back toward the barkeep, when he said, "Well, Wilson, knowing what this boy sprung from, what kind of a man his father was regardless of what the boy says, or his mother, "I'll bet this roll of bills I got stashed in my pocket here," and he squeezed a round and clumsy pocketful of something that could have been a roll of bills, "against the roll you got stashed in your pocket, that he would have shot to kill you with a single round in the forehead without blinking his eye, that is if you are man enough to back up your own words."

Without hesitation, his honor and reputation at put stake by a dinky sheriff and a dinky kid in a dinky trail town in Texas near the border with Mexico, jammed his hand into his pocket, even as the sheriff dumped a roll of greenbacks onto the bar top, and slammed his own roll of money onto the bar right beside that of Sheriff Chuck Turner's roll.

And there in the middle of his roll, as if on historical display, was Jefferson Davis, almost smiling, on a Greyback $50 bill, not a mark of use on it, new as if just minted, bank-stuff only.

The Wagon Master Finds a Lady

And now, for all his good behavior promises, one of the women sat in his mind from the first moment he had seen her. All of it might have been coming down to this first look, all the way from the old country, across the great water, the ship in constant turmoil; atop the waves, and even below deck, with him as a youngster often hidden in secret places by an old sailor with sea-going sons of his own.

She had spoken first; "What did you do before this, Mr. Greenspan, or were you always at this kind of work? My husband can do most anything with his hands." It was a proper introduction and championed her man as they pointed towards Oregon.

Valter Greenspan, a wagon master heading west again, was, at one time, old before his time. His story shouldn't be told to her so early, but he yearned to tell her. She was accessible, curious, sociable at a good scale.

"Here I am, in a warm spring of 1868, about to start on my fourth trip west as a wagon master, this time out of western Pennsylvania, long after my overseas trip from my Jewish homeland in the Near East, looking casually at the host of ladies bound for the spaces on this newest trip yonder. My eyes have lit up at the measurement of talent, beauty and availability of the ladies venturing under my control. Some ladies, on the earlier trips, did not survive the rugged ordeal. Some of those faces could halt my rides, if I let them, if I paused to deliberate, dream a bit. There have been instances where they kept me going, to the next step of these journeys."

He did not tell her the western plains, evident from the outset, had drawn him like a magnet, their open stretches, the plain, green miles of them, as if his mind made easy acceptance of all the clear stretches of the prairies. Greenspan was *his* name, quickly part of America's mix from the Ashkenazic Jewish ornamental surname of *Grünspan*, which undoubtedly came from German *Grünspan 'verdigris' (Middle High German gruenspan)*, borrowed from medieval *Latin viride hispanicum* and meaning *'Spanish green.')*. It would be too much for the lady, a good looker if he ever saw one.

At 45, Greenspan felt at home on the wide spaces of this new country, immeasurable years from the old land where his father ushered him elsewhere. "The old world seeking new gains," his father said, seeing him off on his endless journey. "See me at the end," he added at their parting, his eyes drifting, a hand on the youngster's shoulder for the last time.

In his sleep, or on a hard ride, he'd feel the weight of that hand, the warmth of it, in spite of the years since departure.

Parting, he learned, must be absorbed, or it overruns the soul.

He assumed all women heading out had understood their chances from the outset, their dreams of a new life with their man, for all of them were attached to the man of their choice, or so it appeared to be. They had dreams, hopes, and visions galore, along with a hard-fisted desire to succeed on their mission: it was so simple, there *was* a place waiting for all of them, out and beyond, and that is what brought him and them together for this new trip of his, this fourth journey into the *known unknown,* as he would point out to new comers who carried questions.

They deserved the warning, from a Hebrew sailor turned wagon master, who sailed to Boston from the warring territories of the Near East, sea life traded for life on the trail; Indians, brigands alone and in bands looking for the easy life. Many of their kind he had met, had seen in operation, could detect them early, and up close, he believed, by their eyes, stories told by a wink, a shift of view, and rarely clamped shut.

This new sparkler, Charlotte Kenwood, possibly half the age of her husband Henry, a robust, forward-looking man, wide of shoulder, arm-strength almost visible, willing to do any task regardless of muck or mire, slop or slew, and quick and thorough at fixing wagons as well as horses. Greenspan wondered how Kenwood was with women, with this woman who had caught his own eye out of the lot in the fold. He'd keep a keen eye on both of them.

All of them deserved a look and a judgment; it was a wagon master's responsibility.

And of course, it was Henry Kenwood who said, "I hope they all got sense enough to carry an extra wheel, or even two. It sure would make any job easier, including mine, 'cause I figure much of that is coming my way listening to some others talk about *he can fix anything,* and I know they're talking about me saying that."

He was right on the button with that interpretation, right on the button. And the wagon master brought back visions of leaving a wagon, two wheels broken for good, on the side of a trail, folks trying to save what they could on other wagons, small treasures of seeds and clothes and spinning wheels, and the whole future of a family at sudden odds with life on the move.

Greenspan tried to recount the deserted wagons on those other waysides and gave it up in a hurry in a search for new confidence. That was a demand uppermost in his make-up; *keep 'em happy, keep 'em sure, keep 'em moving.*

But he also knew life had its ebbs and swings coming his way as well as the departures.

Charlotte's looking at him, as often as she did, made things pleasant for a loner, saying unwritten messages, marking places on his heart, perhaps on her own heart. It was guesswork at his best, so, he kept up the chatter when he could.

"You watch where you're going, Miss Charlotte. Some loose rocks up ahead." She'd smile at such approaches, the special care she could make of it, not caring who saw how she smiled back at him, saying, "I won't break any bones, if I can help it. No slowing you down because of me."

She kept pace with him, for him; it was easy to see; and to hear teasing innuendos freely tossed about.

In two weeks, he figured the wagon train had moved about 200 miles. "Not too bad," he calculated, "for people to march beside or behind their wagons, adventurous kin, women and older children, the odd straggler helped when needed."

One of his now-and-then declarations, when some folks might be losing their grip, was a steady-as-you-go promise of, "We are a team and we will finish our mission as a team, the god of Gods be with us."

He told her husband in a trailside talk, one of the few men he cottoned to, other than in harsh or hard commands, "I figure 160 days on the trail, Henry, plus breakdowns, Indians, robberies, sickness of a sort to contend with, that much adding up to 190 days. Of course, I might add, I could be off by half a year. The trip is that contentious, dangers everywhere. If I allow it to bother me, it's like being aboard ship again, problems every which way I turn, and the threats are continual."

Henry made his own observation: "You know a hell of a lot more than we do, Valter, and I hope a bunch of the others understand what's ahead, but not all the possibilities. Some of them might not take another step, them needing your voice in their ears all the time. Charlotte fully understands everything."

He was no part a fool, Greenspan decided.

The two of them were packing some firewood on a pair of donkeys, when they saw a party of riders, just below the horizon, moving at a slow pace, otherwise undetected, heading toward the wagon train.

Tapping Greenspan on the shoulder, Kenwood said, "How do we handle this, Valter? They're organized and surely up to no good way out here."

"We let them get their act together when they brace the train, if that's what they're up to, and I figure, just like you, that's what they're up to. They draw down on the train, we come up behind them, knock off a couple of them, reduce the odds, drive them away with help from the members of the train, coming out of their surprise. I've seen it before, sort of like that."

It went as Valter Greenspan had pictured it; the brigands drew down on the wagon train, had all men, most all men, banded into a circle, when the wagon master and his ally aimed at the group, fired, and dropped three men right off their saddles. The rest scampered off, not to be seen again.

"You got the leader, Valter, because I picked on the oldest looking guy in the bunch, figuring he might really be the brains of the organization. We sure gave that company a frightful greeting."

The pair were treated like heroes by all the members of the wagon train. A banjo broke into song that night, then a guitar. From horizon to horizon, the stars shone at each end of this wide Earth.

The next day, the train moved out, leaving three graves behind them.

Instead of Charlotte hurting her ankle on the rocky trail, the first wheel broke on the number 4 wagon, tossing various goods off the tail end, amid curses galore from the wagon owner who had to unload a goodly amount of supplies to free the spare wheel from its storage.

Greenspan, hearing the curses, rode up and said, "When it's available, we'll have some help here to jack-up the rear end and put on the spare wheel. Save the broken wheel, rim, hub and spokes, for future work. Never can tell when we might need some spare pieces."

Both Henry and Charlotte Kenwood were on the scene in a hurry, using a rugged hand jack to get the wagon lifted. The pair worked like stevedores at the task, Charlotte's smile not hidden at all, and the wagon master could not help the good feelings running through him. He wondered how much it showed, who knew besides her husband? We need each other, he must have been thinking, the three of us. At arrival, it could become a topic of conversation, so, he'd just start over and return to the East, without someone else's wife. It wouldn't matter.

Three weeks later, a Sioux party of warriors attacked the train, both parties having fatalities, and one of them was Henry Kenwood, shot with an arrow directly in his back as he scrambled toward safety with a youngster in his arms. Greenspan pulled the youngster to cover and then went back to retrieve the body of Henry Kenwood. Misery hit him full force and he could not face Charlotte, even at the hastily arranged grave site where she stood with bowed head in prayer or deep sorrow, or both feelings settling about her sure as pain lingers when its signs fly off, like a bird takes flight or a fish escapes a hook, a simple adieu.

The pace of the wagon train put them close to the middle of the country, and Charlotte stayed out of his way, the smiles seemingly gone forever, his deed undone, his small joys crushed, the dreams gone.

It was more than a month later, in the black of night, she slipped under his wagon where he slept on a canvas spread wheel to wheel. "We never made love, Henry and I, not once. He just wanted to get me safely to Oregon to join my folks. He understood we, you and I, had an attraction. I'm sorry it had to come to this, but from the first moment, I knew you were the love I've been waiting for. Please don't hate me. I couldn't stand it. These past weeks have been Hell for me, I swear."

She rolled into his arms. They couldn't see the stars were shining brighter than ever.

Call Me Chef

For the second time this day and for the second day in a row, he looked out the window of the A&P Railroad Lines dining car kitchen in the middle of grass running for endless miles and saw the herd of cattle and the drovers dashing about on horseback, those gallant riders that had drawn him all the way from Italy, half a turn around the world.

Salvatore "Sardi" Benevento, "the best cook on the whole damned railroad," according to the big boss, felt the knot working in his gut. Out there in that mix is where he wanted to be, had wanted it from the day he left Italy with the dream locked up in his heart.

He recalled the exact moment when he sold the horse, the wagon, and the small farm on the same day his grandfather died. Once he arrived in Naples, after the funeral and after his beloved grandfather was placed down into the rocky ground, he purchased a ticket to America. A few months later, after an interminable wait, and a mad and dangerous crossing of the ocean among some thieves from his own village, he managed to maintain his inner direction, to keep his dream alive.

Ashore but one week, exploring Boston's North End on foot, he felt like a child away from home. But he glowed in the energy bouncing around him. Like a small piece of Italy that part of Boston came at him in its full swing. In the air were the known aromas of hours' long food preparation, the sense of music from every corner and from every bistro, from open windows and closed doors, and finally the magnificent chatter of its people, dialect atop dialect, a grand mixture of Tuscany tongue and Calabrese and Milanese and Roman as old as the sages. He inhaled all of it, as if hunger worked all the parts of him.

Then, fate itself on the move, in one breath, not marked right then but benchmarked later in the way life piles up with incidents, he heard a voice saying in a dialect near his own from the front of an open restaurant, *"Ho, Luigi, perché una tale pesante, sguardo interrogativo sulla tua faccia? Si guarda sbalordito."* He had no trouble hearing it as, "Ho, Luigi, why do you have such a heavy, quizzical look on your face? You look dumbfounded."

The speaker was a heavy, well-set man of middle age, mustache-bearing, dark of skin, in a fashionable black suit with simple orange stripes behaving in the fabric like style was its master. The felt hat on his head seemed as new as Benevento knew the suit was, and somewhat costly even in the land of riches. The speaker's hands flew in the air as he talked, approaching an obvious acquaintance at an outside table.

The one he spoke to, Luigi as named, replied, *"Ho bisogno di trovare un grande cuoco italiano, un cuoco supremo, un maestro del gusto, per la ferrovia."* ("I need to find a great Italian cook, a chef supreme, and a master of taste, for the railroad.")

Young Benevento, having been taught everything his grandfather knew about meats and vegetables in the kitchen, the best seasons of vegetables, the uses of condiments, the difference in minute mixtures, "the splash and dash" he might have called it, how soft the fruits could become in the mouth, in the throat, stepped in as quickly as he had sold the horse and wagon and the farm. He burst into Italian, went immediately to English to carry his argument, to show his versatility. "Call me Chef," he cried out. "I am he whom you are looking for. This is the moment I have been waiting for. The Good Lord sent me down this street on this day to show how destiny works at His hands through these hands." He pointed overhead and blessed himself.

"I am the best cook, the best chef, ever to come out of the mountains in Tuscany. I sold my horse and wagon and farm to get here to America, to bring great Italian cooking to the new land of America. I am Salvatore Benevento at your service. Ask the proprietor to loan me his kitchen for an hour. I shall make your mouths water, make you think of home so that you will cry for your mother's kitchen. Blessed be the image that comes upon you now from your childhood." He made the sign of the cross over them as if he was the village padre.

The two older Italian men, marveling at such precocity in the young man, tumbled before his onslaught. He told them how his grandfather had cooked for years for the two of them and for every celebration in their small village. He spelled out some of his own favorite recipes that moved both men to salivation, and to a few more times of their calling out to the proprietor, "another round of vino for us and the young man, Giovanni, if you please." *("Un altro giro di vino per noi e il giovane, Giovanni, se non vi dispiace.")*

The proprietor, after all the talk and Benevento being hired on the spot for the chef's position on a train leaving the next day for the far western lands of America, finally asked him what he would have cooked if he had been given the run of the restaurant kitchen. The proprietor's eyes were wide with anticipation.

"Ah, I immediately thought of mushroom *trifoliate*," Benevento said, "for a late afternoon delicacy for these men of taste, most tasty sautéed mushrooms."

The proprietor looked downcast as he said, "That would have been impossible, young man, as we do not have any mushrooms in the kitchen today." He dropped his shoulders as he looked at the others, his hands flung out flat at the imagined loss.

But they all brightened as the young chef looked overhead at a string of tall elm trees, and said, "That is no problem. The Garden in the Sky above us is filled with amanita colyptraderma the Good Lord has provided us. Look at the parade of those choice mushrooms along the upper branch in that large tree across the street. Do they not look delicious even from here?"

Salvatore Benevento, the very next day, was chef No. 1 in the dining car of an A&P Railroad Lines passenger train heading west out of Boston, Tuscany fare on the move.

Nobody yet in the new land realized his real dream was to be a cowboy.

His number 2 cook, Giovanni Ciampa, said one day, as the train left one stop and started on its way again, "I do not poke my nose in your business, Sardi, but I notice you skip out at each stop to buy small things for yourself or perhaps for a lady friend. Can I help with anything? Romance for itinerants like us is a problem from the very beginning."

"Ah, Joe, you I trust to the utmost I'll ask you right up front to keep my secret always. I have taken this job to become, one day in my dreams, a cowboy. It has driven me since I first heard about them. The stories, the legends, the whole drama of the west as it changes the country feeding it. Yes, the things I buy, the things I keep in my personal bag, are things that I will need as a cowboy. I can't make the change dressed like this." He swept his hands down his cook's attire, the floury sleeves, the apron already having its share of bright juices and liquids and sweeping stains where he wiped his wrists in a hurry. "Ah, no, never dressed like this. This is not a cowboy." There was disgust in his voice that Giovanni understood.

Seven trips Benevento made back and forth across the great country, across the great river, saw Chicago and St. Louis and burgeoning towns and settlements in Texas and along the Rocky Mountains. It was easy to keep his dream alive for continually he saw from the train windows the herds moving on the wide grasslands or finally corralled for rail movement and saw the cowboys at every drive's end clearing their dry mouths, cutting the trail dust in their throats, relaxing as if relaxing was a brand-new thing for them. He was caught up in the excitement of their world, those simple successes after fraught perils only special men could survive.

In the midst of his eighth trip on the railroad, in an overnight stop in Colorado, he planned to step off the train just after midnight, when the whole world seemed asleep, when deep dreams were at hand.

On his way to the door, silence everywhere like a silken mist, he touched Giovanni on the cheek to waken him.

"Joe," he said in a whisper, and getting Joe's attention. "This is where I get off. This is where I become a cowboy. Wish me luck, my friend. I have written a note to the owners saying that you are the best man for the job now. You know all that I have taught you, all that my grandfather taught me. Speak up when you want to make a point. Trust the taste on your lips. Don't take a back seat for anybody on the train or in the big offices. You are a good chef. I hope to become as good a cowboy, but we'll let time do the talking there. Be well, my friend. *Buona fortuna. Arrivederci.*"

He swung his personal bag over his shoulder, heard the tinny rattle of its contents, and stepped into darkness and a new world. In the morning, from an old man at a livery stable with a crude sign saying "Horses for sale," he bought a horse and a saddle and started to learn how to ride. Benevento was a good learner and handled the horse quickly. Two days later he sought employment from a trail boss whose herd was resting a few miles back on the prairie.

"You look brand new. Is them duds you're wearing that new they look like they wasn't worn anyplace yet? Who'd you work for last? You ever drove herd?"

"Well," Benevento said, "I can ride that horse of mine all day."

"Who'd you work for afore this?" the trail boss asked. "Can you rope, pull out a dogie for chow, run down a runaway and bring it back? You ain't lookin' the type."

"This will be my first job, but I have read everything about cowboys and I know I can do the job. I came all the way from Italy to be a cowboy." The pain and the dream were both in his face.

"Oh, boy," the trail boss said, "I got a dreamer here on my hands." He snorted and thought a bit and said, "The only thing I got right now is a sick cookie who's ailin' and abed in the chuck wagon. If you can heat beans and water and make the coffee, you got a job until he gets better. Then, when that's scored up, we'll see how good you done. You game for that? What's your name?"

"Sardi Benevento, and I can cook anything. I can make your mouth water from half a mile. All I want is a chance to be a cowboy when your cook gets better. You help me and I'll help you."

"That's a deal, Sardi. Follow me." And he led him to his herd at a sit-down a few miles out on the grass.

It took one meal and the whole crew of drovers knew they had a "chef" working the chuck wagon. He plain outdid himself and the sick cook in that first meal, his personal bag of supplies coming up as handy as a can opener. From then on, anytime a drover or ramrod or the trail boss went into town, Benevento made sure they had a list of condiments and vegetables that he'd put on a list for them. Every purchase made his cooking tasks much easier.

The night the top wrangler came back with a half barrel of apples, Benevento promised them apple pie for a late snack. By darkness he had all hands drooling for the dessert. He surprised them at camp by unpacking his reflector oven, a shiny tin contraption, from his personal bag and erecting it in front of the open fire. Flames seemed to leap into its parts.

He went to work at his fold down table at the rear of the wagon. Soon, cinnamon swimming in the air, sugar coming sweet as honey bread, he had his first apple pie in the oven and the aroma raced across the grass. Night riders on the far edges of the herd were afraid they'd be left out, but there was plenty of apple pie for all of them, the fire hot for hours, the oven soaking up the direct heat, night filling up with the absolute sweetness sitting in the air. In addition, as an extra part of his dessert, he prepared a special sauce to top the slabs of apple pie. The night was lustrous.

Two days later the original cook was back on the job and Benevento had his first turn as a drover.

The trail boss, Max Farmer, said, "Sardi, you're one helluva cook. But a promise is a promise, so you get your shot at bein' a cowpoke, not that I think there's any more glory in it than bein' a great cook. I gotta tell you to keep awake on the night rounds. Sing sweet and low, like one of your nice goodies, and don't close your eyes. We got strange goin's on in this territory. There's always somethin' goin' on out here two ways if you was to look twice."

So, Benevento sang lightly, sweetly, a soft tenor; "Sleep little babies, sleep on my side. Sleep, little dogies, sleep as I ride." It came out as, *"Dormi bambino, dormi su un fianco. cani poco sonno, sonno come io giro."*

He sang sweetly, soft as a nightingale in the shadows, and the small speck of light he spied at a distant point was minute, almost insignificant, like a firefly at work, but he had seen no fireflies yet, and decided to wander over that way.

With his horse tied off on some brush, he slipped into a swale and made his way to where the light had been seen. There came the snicker of a horse and the covered cough of a man on a small hummock. The man, obviously, was watching the herd and any other activity. He coughed again and never heard Benevento sneak up behind him and stick the stiletto he'd carried forever against the other man's throat.

"Say nothing, *Signore*, or you are dead," Benevento said. "Walk with me, walk quietly to your horse. You make one move and I will sink the blade into your throat. You will never make noise again. Never sing. Never say hello or goodbye to any loved one." He nudged the knife point a bit tighter against the throat of the man.

"You understand me?"

"Yes. Don't cut me. I won't do anything."

Benevento led the man to his own horse, unhooked his lasso, and tied the man up. Then he walked him to the man's horse and had him climb into the saddle, still tied up. That is the way the night camp guard saw them coming into firelight and called Max Farmer, the trail boss. "Hey, Max, we got company coming in with the Sardi the cook."

Farmer asked the man many questions and got no answers. He repeated many of the questions, the firelight reflecting on the man's face, and the fear showing in his eyes.

From the edge of the firelight, from the edge of darkness, Benevento, the just replaced cook, walked to the chuck wagon and from his bag retrieved a small honing stone. At the campfire, in view of the captured lookout, whose hands were still bound, Benevento started sharpening his stiletto. The keen knife edge was slowly drawn across the stone, the whisper of the fine abrasion circulating in the air as thin as a bird's wings. Slowly, again and again, he drew the blade and the shiny tip across the stone. He kept thinking about the whir of a hummingbird's wings.

"Perhaps, Boss, you might give me an opportunity to pose some questions to him." He didn't wait for an answer from Farmer but drew up a sitting box and sat directly in front of the captured lookout.

"You and I have had a discussion, haven't we, *Signore*? We spoke of small things, didn't we, *Signore?* Shall we start again with some more questions?"

The trussed man, in the light of the fire, under the eyes of a dozen men, with Benevento and the stiletto yet making slight but serious sounds in the night like the mystical threat of a hummingbird, came loose at every seam. He told them everything he knew; how many men they had in their rustler's gang, who the leader was, when and how they planned to kill as many men as quickly as they could and then to stampede the herd. Later on, they would have the forces to regroup the herd and make off with it.

"Well," Farmer said after he heard the whole story, "maybe we can do a little surprise on our own. We'll just go over there and shoot up that whole camp of rustlers as fast as we can. Scatter them to the winds and all the hills." He was not a big man but he had the big word.

That is, until the former cook and cowboy, Sardi Benevento, said, "Why endanger any of our men with that effort, Mr. Farmer? Why don't we get the herd as close as we can in the night, while they're all sleeping and stampede the herd right through their hideout? That should soften things up for us. And we'll do the regrouping."

"Why, *Signore,*" Farmer said, "you are no longer a cook in this here outfit. You are now lead scout and a full-blown cowboy. But if I was you, I wouldn't throw away that shiny tin oven of yours."

Greg Knighthawk, Sheriff, Taxico County

Gregory George "Greg" Knighthawk was a Kootenai Indian, Northern Idaho branch, and the first Indian or tribal sheriff in Taxico County, Idaho. Even today, 140 years after his death, he is still part of everyday discussions among the remaining members of the Kootenai tribe. I first heard about him from a comrade in the Korean campaign in 1951-1952, in the 31st Infantry Regiment, near Lake Hwachon, where life and death came by the numbers.

"They didn't know, not at first, that he was an Indian, a Kootenai Indian, when they made him sheriff, and he was so good at his job, that they forgot about his past in a hurry." These words came to me in a foxhole with Elliot "Chief" Hillborn, a corporal in my squad, the gutsiest man I ever met, out to prove something to somebody, for sure.

I'm sure they talk about him, too.

Chief said, "Some townsmen saw him attack three men who were going to abuse a woman whose husband they had just shot dead from ambush. He killed all three opponents, freed the woman, and accepted on the spot the badge they offered him, making him sheriff of Taxico County, Idaho in 1878. He served but a year on the job before he was shot from behind by six men from a prison break.

"The good parts," added Chief, "are the ones in between, like three days on the job and the bank is robbed and he doesn't kill the robbers, but disables each one and disarms each one and locks each one in a cell, then counted out the money recovered to the bank president in front of the whole town. Don't bother trying to tell me that doesn't make a big on-the-spot splash for customers of the bank, never-you-mind the banker himself."

I thought it was one helluva story, and told Chief how it hit me.

It brought a smile to Chief's face, and then he plusses it with another lulu. "That's not the end of it. A week later, another gang tries to rob the bank and the sheriff ends up having to shoot three robbers, and then he again counts out the money for the banker in front of the whole town, and this time, believe me or not, there's half as much in the pile as counted out the first time. He arrests the banker on the same damned spot. After a long search, he finds the balance of money in the banker's barn, stashed up in the loft under some hay. Knighthawk's from then on a hero to everybody."

Chief and I had some real action then, of our own, and he's the master not only of his rifle bayonet but a hand-knife some magician must have made and blessed 'cause it's got miracles in it, on it, all over it. Saved my bacon, he did, for the next breakfast on the side of the mountain. I'm chewing all the time and he's spewing about the Kootenai Indians and their very special roles in life, way back when right up to now, and the miracles are evident.

"Keep me handy," he says, casual as all outdoors, but probably meaning it to the core of the matter. "We have our destinies just like Knighthawk did, and we have to keep our appointments with Time."

There was a sort of spiritual revelation at that moment, and it came to me as the very Lord's truth, the pair of them in closer contact than I could realize.

I finally said, after a bit more palaver, "How did he die?"

"Oh," Chief replied, "you rush toward the end too quickly. Enjoy the revelations, the spirit of a special man, a special Kootenai Indian right from his very start, when his mother said, every tie asked, that she was a virgin and never touched by man, Kootenai Indian or white man, never once."

"Oh," I leaped in with, "that can't be. You know that."

"You saying it could never happen? Not in all our times, not in all of histories of man? Are you telling me that Knighthawk was just a man born to be good at whatever, or that he was special? If he was special, then all the facts about him could be as we believe them to be, as we Kootenai Indians believe them to be?"

The pride practically rang in his voice, coming so loud and sure it almost knocked me over. I was in the company of a special man, and it brought, almost to life, a sense of what it was like way back when Knighthawk was making his solid way in a white man's world, short though it was. I tried to recall any Indians which had the same impact and their names leaped at me in a rush, and with a few surprises in the mix, like Will Rogers. I guessed at them being peacemaker, but they came as warriors, for sure, a host of leaders in America: Cochise, Crazy Horse, Geronimo, Red Cloud, Pontiac, Squanto, Tecumseh, Sitting Bull, right into the movies that kept them somewhat alive, at least their being made aware of.

Almost at the same time, I was aware of what most of us do not know nor ever cares. But history has a way of coming back on one's ignorance of it, a special compilation and awareness of footsteps in all the ages of man that retain proper names of most proper men, proper heroes. They start, incidentally, when somebody speaks the name of such a person; asks a question, reads a quote, hears a loud exclamation of greatness never before brought to mind, but is there, forever, for the grasping, like someone saying to me, down the road away, "Have you ever heard of Knighthawk, Chief of the Kootenai Indians?"

Near asleep, one of those deadly nights, images at a gallop in my mind, seeking resolution, truth, the next statement rich with a kind of hunger, a slash of sustenance, I found Knighthawk in my head, no tomahawk in his hand, no bow and arrow, no silky maiden of the tribe making advances, no target in his mind that I could invent. He came forward, not in stealth but eagerness to clasp my hand, and I could not refuse his reach.

Pete Rowes and the Way It Goes

Compton Hills, Idaho was in turmoil, ranchers being robbed, cattle rustled, women abused, a whole gamut of sins and terrors being dropped on its people by one or more gangs, but nobody was sure. Who was what? The lone sheriff, Otto Klinger, was desperate for help, but two deputies had been killed in the line of duty, and no one else stepped up for a badge.

Things had to change, and Klinger kept looking.

Accidents, we know, happen in life, both the good and the bad, and we must be ready and wary about which is what, how we meet such circumstances, opportunities, which way we should turn.

Pete Rowes, for your information, played the uke, the guitar, and sang songs like a natural crooner, all which enhanced his charm with the women of the west, and all other points of the compass you can possibly think of. As such, he rode into Compton Hills, Idaho, one day with all his gear hanging on for the ride; both the uke and the guitar on slings across the back of the saddle and his charm upright on the back of a stallion black as Hades' promise. He had a pleasant face most folks would call handsome, his nose was still straight and unbroken, golden hair protruded about his ears in a curly and likeable fashion, and he moved like music itself, every note of it, smooth as a violin can be.

Women of the town, ladies and otherwise, noticed him from squeezed-in little patios, and doors of every kind open on buildings of every kind. The men of the town also noted his entry, including sheriff Otto Klinger, ten years on the job and a keen eye at marking men for what they most likely were or meant to be, like cowpokes looking for work, adventurers of any ilk, troubles for bartenders or ladies, and trouble for him personally, all of them sooner or later in contact with the sheriff for reasons of discontent, theft, murder, and loud music too early in the morning or too late at night.

"Hell," Klinger said aloud with nobody in his small office with him, "this one looks like the whole orchestra itself." He was fed quick images of a strummer at the only saloon in town, and then at a peaceful campfire out on the grass, or sitting on a lady's patio or front porch. The last was the strongest and stayed with him longer than the other images. "But I'm already casing him for somethin' else, even though he's some momma's little boy just growed up." He often found temperance in his own words.

The sheriff watched the newcomer slide off the saddle, grab his guitar and sidle through the open door of the Bull's Horn Saloon, the lone saloon. "I'd best go see him play for his first drink," Klinger said aloud, adding to his morning dialogue, "might be damned well entertaining."

He somehow brought up the image of the stranger riding on the hot grass of the Idaho plains area, his throat dry as old cow bones or scratchy as a desert elsewhere on his journey, and the back of his neck, below his sombrero, still prickly red from the eternal prairie sun. To a point, there was really nothing else to separate him from any other stranger come to Compton Hills.

At the same moment, on the second floor of the saloon, he spotted Mother Marylou, a long-known acquaintance, summon one of her charges to note the stranger's arrival, and likely the swing of his guitar, the sway of his hips, he was willing to bet. But that's when he also first saw the slight rhythm of a holstered pistol on the stranger's hip, low, loose, with a rhythm of its own, a gunfighter's rhythm.

Now, he realized, he had a double interest. His mind could not bring back any poster of a gunner with a guitar; they sure did not mix.

The sheriff slopped on his sombrero, his two pistols, straightened his shirt collar, made sure each shirt button was in place. In time, he knew he'd swap details with Marylou.

There was no surprise as the pleasant voice in a pleasant song came to him as he neared the saloon doors swung wide open to the day. "Already at work for his first drink," he judged for himself, and swiftly asked himself, "I wonder if he's that fast with his guns." The sidearms moved with the rhythm generated by the song, and Klinger had a quick image fly across his forehead of the stranger in another kind of quickness. Neither was he surprised at this event.

When the song was finished, Jocko the barkeep and saloon owner, slid a drink in front of the singer.

Klinger, from a short distance and with a calm voice, asked, "Have I ever met you, son? Do you know me, the local sheriff, a music lover from way back east in Tennessee, a stickler for reading wanted posters, every one of 'em come to my attention? You ever on any of 'em? I am thinkin' I seen your face before, someplace, somewhere. Was it on a wanted poster? I'd like to know who's in my town, what brought 'em here, where they headed when they leave. If we get that all squared away to my satisfaction, you can keep on singin' all day and all night if Jocko here don't mind it. I sure don't mind it. You got a great voice, son, a great voice. You that good with 'em guns you're sportin' right now?"

It was a staggering amount of talk, loaded with questions waiting answers, all the customers in the saloon at close attention to the open discussion brought to point.

A near-liquid response came from the stranger, "No, sir, never made any of those posters you're talking about, not a single one. But I can shoot these pistols just as good as I can sing my songs, quick, sure, straight with an aim for whatever, and can keep doing it as fast as needed in every case. My name is Pete Rowes, that's how it goes, no matter where I'm at or what I'm doing."

Klinger could not hold back his sudden fervor. "You lookin' for work, son? You ever consider workin' for the law? Bein' a deputy. I need a deputy right up front right now, if you're of a mind to do so."

"Well, after we discuss private stuff without all the ears, you can explain a few things to me, like pay, a place to bunk, a few introductions to special folks in town like Jocko whom I've already met and that lady across the street still gawking at us as we discuss employment. She always that curious?"

After a private discussion, Klinger told his new hire, "Tomorrow we start a new campaign. Somebody here in town keeps tabs on me, and now on us, for whoever runs this wild bunch that's raisin' hell all around. In the mornin', town awake, we ride out of town, you heading east and me west. We circle way out of town and meet at the foot of Eagle Hill, north of us. You can't miss it. From there we'll have a look at the three hills out there. For sure, the good ole bad boys gotta have a bunkin' place to spend their nights, and we can catch 'em in a damned good crossfire."

He tossed a rifle at Rowes and said, "I hope you're as good with this as you are with them guns of your'n."

"Just a couple shots better at long range, dead on target," Rowes tossed in with solid comfort. "I don't miss what I shoot at, 'specially with a new rifle like this one. And I want a whole bankroll of ammo."

"You'll have all I got, son. Best I can do."

The pair left in the morning, both from the sheriff's office and jail, in full view of the town, heading east and heading west in no great hurry, Hours later they rendezvoused at Eagle Hill.

At the second hill inspected, they saw a single rider come likely from town into a gully. A checkout revealed a small cabin, a dozen horses tied off at a rail, and an occasional cowpoke visit an outhouse. The rider just arrived remounted his horse and headed back, presumably, they figured, to town.

Klinger asked his new deputy, at two dollars a day, what he thought should be the first thing to do.

Rowes answered immediately; "Scatter the horses, every one of them. A few rounds popping under them should take care of that."

Klinger said, "We'll need some horses to get them back to town."

Rowes said, "There won't be too many to worry about, but we have to wait until that rider is far enough away not to hear our barrage,"

"Another half hour," Klinger said, "and the hills will hold it all in." He studied Rowes face and asked, "You never did any of this before?"

"Nope," came Rowes answer, but I read a lot whenever I can get a magazine or newspaper, and all this has been done before, done and written about. Now, we about ready?"

His first round, under the cluster if horses, broke loose every horse into a scrambled run down the valley floor.

In half an hour, a white flag waved at them from the front door of the cabin, and three men walked out, and were ordered to stand aside while the deputy slammed six more shots into the cabin, before a fourth man walked out, his hat waving his way free from the firing.

Manacled, roped, the four men were hustled into more ropes, with one man designated to bury the dead in a patch of ground beside the littered cabin. It took a few hours, in which four horses were recaptured for the ride back to Compton Hills jail, the new deputy still thinking about the nosy but buxom lady on the upper porch across from The Bull's Horn Saloon.

The Cowtown Candlemaker

"You blow out that candle, pardner, and we'll be in the dark 'til kingdom comes. No two ways about it."

"Hell, just light it up again."

"I don't have no more matches. You carryin' any?"

"Not a one. How'd you get hold of a candle?"

"I always carry one in the crown of my sombrero. You could say I have a history with candles, so don't blow out that candle or we'll never get out of this cave. Why'd ya think they stuck us in here, for fun? Those Indians mean business all the way through, and they are a funny bunch to boot."

"How do we get out of here? And they got our horses, too. We could never just walk away even if we get out of here." The despondency showed sure in his voice.

The tallest man of the two, Chuck Collins, said to the other gent, Pete Marvin, "Them's some weird injuns who don't even take our guns, and they sure think we'll never get out on our own. This place is probably their first home, before any of us come this far west. They're older than the hills, I'll wager." There was sufficient curiosity in his voice that dwarfed any fear, as though he was poised enough to take on whatever came up in his way.

"Well, I'm the one they wanted, Pete, and you just happened to be near me, so you got grabbed too. You could say that was your bad luck, but I don't carry good luck like it's in my saddlebag or sittin' the saddle with me. Luck is made by yourselves in most matters, and you can take that to your next session of doubt."

"Whatta they want with you? You got no gold, no money, Hell, not any matches either. Why's that? Whattayou got they want?"

"I make better candles than they do, simple as that, so they're doing it this way to see how I make my candles so good, least better than the one's they make, and then steal my idea. Steal my candles too."

"What makes this candle so much better than their candles? A candle's just a damned candle far as I see it." He chuckled at his own joke, but halfheartedly at that. It really said he wanted to know the difference in candles, as far as he could see. It seemed so silly to hm, yet here he was in a cave without his horse but had his guns, and with a man who called himself just a plain old candlemaker. He tried to reach for some old dreams sitting on the edge of his mind, but nothing surfaced.

"I make my candles with beeswax," Collins said, his voice suddenly mysterious, "and not plain old animal fat or tallow like they use.

My candles last longer, throw light better, make it worth the while for all the differences twixt the two kinds."

"This candle doesn't shine any deeper in this cave, that I see, so what's that gain us?"

"We'll have light longer than they think we will. They probably don't think of it that way, just that we'll die eventually in here without anything to eat, and they'll just walk in here then and scoop up anything and everything we have, including the makings of my kind of candle. It's plain as all that."

The candleholder nearly tripped, nearly dropped the candle. Shadows flickered on the wall of the cave with that misstep.

"Like I said, Pete, don't let that one go out 'cause we'd just stumble around in here until we die."

Pete Marvin, a plain old cowboy, almost not believing the stories being told him by this still alive candlemaker, this obviously plain old cowboy named Chuck Collins. They had plain bumped into each other on the trail. Now he thought he best listen to this other man who'd done more things than him, knew his way around in the dark, so it seemed, and who might, even now, have an idea on how to get out of this fix, this dark cave that might have no other way in or out except the one they used to get away from a band of Indians chasing them right into the mouth of this cave, this tomb of tombs.

Marvin, in all reality, feared they were in a prison. And for the rest of their natural lives, until the end of darkness when this single, simple candle burnt down to his fingertips and he'd have to drop it. In a quick turn, he couldn't imagine how much time was allotted to their lives. Darkness, ahead of them, behind them, befuddled him, whereas the new casual friend appeared to be in some control of his own destiny.

Things too big to measure had always bothered him, stretched his mind further than it could go with reason, yet darkness was real, and imprisonment was real and death, of course, was the most real of all possibilities.

It began to crush him. Time began to compress. He could feel the squeeze as it made its way through the cave, just as thick as the darkness.

Then, by all the graces one could muster, a puff of air, fresh as a newborn, touched at the candle in his hand and made it flicker, at which the candlemaker jumped to immediate attention, and said to his companion, "Hold on for dear life, Pete, and go ahead of me down this way," and he pointed into the deepest blackness.

An hour later, as might be guessed, they saw a slim band of light slide out of harsh darkness and elongate itself as tall as they were. It was a tall slice of daylight.

"Now," Chuck Collins said, "snuff out that candle. We wait here until it's dark outside, then we'll get the Hell out of here, find a couple of horses, perhaps our own, and plain skedaddle on our way."

"What should I do with this candle?" Pete Marvin asked, as he wet thumb and forefinger and snuffed out the fluttering flame.

"Toss it in the corner where they won't find it in a hurry. They probably know the difference in makings already, or should by now. It didn't take me long, but the ideas have been around a long time, at least somewhere else besides here with me."

Collins managed to peak around the outside of the cave and when he came back, he said, "You won't believe this, Pete. But our horses are out there in a small village of tepees and saddled up as if they never took those saddles off. And I saw something else very interesting."

He held onto that revelation until Pete said, "What the heck are you talkin' about now, you got me so twisted up I can't think straight."

"There's a huge bee nest they haven't seen yet or just don't pay any attention to, but I'm thinking the bees might just help me, help us, in another way. Let me think about it for a while, then I'll tell you what might get us out of here."

How the heck are bees gonna help us get away? That's all I'm interested in." He leaned back and decided to keep his mouth shut.

An hour later, dusk starting its early invasion into low spots and valleys, and around the small Indian encampment, Chuck Collins flung a stone into the midst of the bee's nest and a cloud of bees flew, like a black cloud, directly at the Indian village.

The Indians fled, the dark cloud of bees buzzing after them like they meant business, and the two cowboys ran out the rear end of the cave, leaped onto their horses and were out of sight in a short haul, not a single bee after them.

"That," Collins said, "is two times bees have had a hand helping me, or a thousand wings."

The Old Man from Dry Harbor

If Jess Perling, bounty hunter supreme, was to tell you his own story, it would read like this:

The whole town figured Jess Perling was the first man to arrive at Dry Harbor, on the edge of the desert, and would be the last to leave. Even at 62, getting long in the tooth, slimmer at the hip so that his gun belt became a shoulder holster. But either way, they also knew he was a dead shot, uphill or down or across the dry sands, out there where some days the sun lit the whole damned desert with fire on its own calling.

As always with heroes of most sorts, the legends carry the message. When Sliver Partridge broke out of the skimpy jail in Dry Harbor, men in the Dry Float Saloon began to create odds that old Jess would collect the reward; hadn't he collected several so far? They had no idea where Jess started, but this time it was in the forest on the other side the hill where he found the stump that had yielded a 4 foot length of 4"x4" beam which had then been inserted into the jail window between bars, laid horizontally across the window and tied to a rope tied to a horse in the dark, all which pulled the wall down, the town still asleep at dawn, Sliver Partridge on the run.

But not too far.

The tracks led him to a cabin on the edge of the desert, to the escapee, the accomplice, the reward. It was as slick as sweat on a man's chest. Jess Perling, pushing hard at 63, at it again! "Bounty hunters' bounty hunter," to say the least.

Jess Perling loomed into saloon discussions when a tall young man rode into town, his face recognizable to the sheriff, the new arrival wearing a pair of holstered pistols as much parts of him as his long arms. Sheriff Deke Morgan walked directly into his office/jail and pulled at a pile of wanted posters, finding Cliff Darwin's handsome face on two circulars, from two sources on two crimes of death at dueling for no good cause, the loophole being understood immediately by the sheriff who knew he had to sit on his knowledge until something happened to light it up. The next local shooting might be a punishable crime.

He hoped the young shooter would not stay long in Dry Harbor.

At the Dry Float Saloon, Darwin, at his first drink, showed he was comfortable in front of a crowd, when he said, "I came here, to this quiet town out of the way of regular long-talk folks who'd rather see a dead duel than a great foot race. Most of them don't care who dies, as long as the excitement is worth it, a close shave with one gun, a deadly hit from the other end. I think a lot of them figure their town ain't been blessed unless they have a duel in the street, a man fall in the dust, a hero to bump a saloon up to proper level, sharing death being part of sharing life, a duel in the street making a town a part of the western mystique. Try selling that to any man dead from a duel."

He drained off his third drink, slid the glass down the bar, almost like saying to the crowd, "I'm at your service."

The barkeep, Ever Slot, slipped him another drink, seeing business was on the upswing. He couldn't agree more with the young shooter. When the cluster around Darwin grew thicker, noisier, drinks practically rolling down the bar top, Slot kept his eyes open for Jess Perling to walk in the open door, check out the commotion, make his way over to Deke Morgan's office and check the wanted posters. Such a step would pay-off in the long run, he assured himself.

It unfolded just that way, as Perling joined the mob at the bar, heard the talk, walked back out the door and went to the sheriff's office. Morgan saw him coming, laid out on his desk the two wanted posters on the young stranger.

"I knew you'd be comin' to see me, Jess, but this kid has a lawful loophole protectin' him." He explained the legal end of the matter to the old bounty hunter, who nodded, agreed, said, "If he behaves himself, we all get a good rest. If he don't, me and you got work on our hands."

Jess Perling rode out of town the same way Cliff Darwin had ridden into town, feeling the connection and the contradiction working on each other in the back of his head, yet squirming in the palms of his hands.

He was halfway out of town when he heard the echo of a shot. He waited for a reply, a retort. None came. There was no scrambling behind him. An image of the Darwin kid showing folks how good he was, probably had been proposed and completed to everybody's satisfaction. Jess kept up on his departure on that realization.

Sleep came to both men, Perling on his own bed in his own cabin, Darwin in a back room at the saloon, Slot figuring it was a good deal for him and the young shooter, who had rung up business a few good notches, and was sure to continue come the new day.

Dawn jumped into bed for most sleepers, making them aware of heat on the quick entry, the search for cover and shade an endless task, wondering how many shelters were in this hot hole of a town, live as coals from an old fire.

He was not in town when cocky Jigs Wentworth came riding in, going directly to the Dry Float Saloon to get a glimpse of the fancy gun shooter he heard was in town casting about his prowess with pistols, spreading his name a few more kilometers and, for sure, drinking all the free booze and beer he wanted in a fair swap of deeds.

The sheriff was one of those men who wondered what the hell had kept him here, made him accept his job in the first place, keep at it for several years. No swift answers came back to him on wonder's journey.

And then he heard that the young cock of the grass, Jiggs Wentworth, had come to Dry Harbor to stir the pot. It was inevitable, he told himself. "Day's just started, or maybe it's near over." The wide brimmed sombrero, almost an umbrella, was scooped off his desk, launched on his head with a "Back to work, I guess. Should have seen it comin'"

He inched his way to the saloon, no hurry in mind, gun silence sitting idly in the air in all parts of Dry Harbor.

He wondered how far away Jess Perling was, his nose working for sure. The sudden memory coming to him of the first time he had seen Jess Perling, smoky gun in hand, a suspected back-shooter dead on the trail just outside of town.

"Gave himself away, Deke. Not knowing I never like anybody riding or hiding behind me on the trail. Caught him when he thought he was goin' to get a bead on me. Not his best day for guessin', was it?"

Turf Malloy's Squeaky Dreams

Thurman "Turf" Malloy, dreamer, supposed cowman, comfortable in the saddle all the live-long day, looked across the Texas plains, his eyes stretching beyond what he saw, not noting the herd of cattle spread across his view. That moment was all of a century and a half ago, 1867 to be exact in our count, and Turf on the search.

"Cattle don't occupy my mind," Turf Malloy'd often say, yet with a knowledgeable nod at an interested face, he'd add, "but what they trample on does, the land occupies my mind. Where puncher cooks cook their steaks keeps telling me there's gold in the land. Not the yellow kind, not the ring and necklace stuff, but that under-earth stuff that'll make empires from down below. Whole vast empires." His hands stretched widely at his sides.

There came a gleam in his smile.

The thought made him nervous, but gave him energy, drove him on.

As it was, near 1643, two centuries earlier, the Indians of western Texas had found fluid coming out of rocks and earth, which they believed was medicinal, and so spun the tales of its power, and thus carried the proof of what had been found. Watercraft of different kinds had also been caulked with the new finding, thereby twisting legend and lore in a couple of directions. Malloy treated such data with the reverence that historians have for the past, sorting fact from fiction, lore from legend when feasible, guess from proof, whenever they could.

It was after the Civil War rocked the land, when Turf Malloy started drilling for oil in 1867, following the suit of other seekers, and kept the empire dream moving on its edges, a capacity of thought working through many of his nights, making dreams, disturbing sleep.

Accidental interruptions can mark most days, and usually toss in extra mixes of every degree for those folks with attention or awareness, or those waiting for charms to work or bad luck to rear its ugly head. Proof of this came on the day he met Alice Hudson and her husband Tim on a rocky trail, their small party already attacked by a few Indians, Tim Hudson sorely wounded, and close to death. Turf Malloy's life took another twist. He ministered as best he could the wounded man who died in his arms, and saw the new widow's sad beauty evolve during that day, a kind of beast and beauty element of itself.

"He was an honest and good man," Alice said in quick surmise, as Turf put a marker on the new grave in the middle of nowhere, mountains and cliffs and rocky stages of erosion abounding in every view as far as one could see and still make judgments, not be awed by the land itself.

Turf replied, "And now you are in my custody from this day onward."

In the morning, they moved on, their searches doubled by trouble, new hungers working, the area known as Hillview directly ahead of them, possibly fortune and future also, and a huge sadness behind them in the rocky ground. For long hours, even her beauty at rest, his eyes scanned the trail, the rims and edges of cliffsides poking their chins and rocky paths at him.

Oil, he was positive of, sat at rest, waiting to be found, ready to pour into a thousand types of containers. Oil was the huge dream. Oil was the fortune waiting for the adventurers, the daring, the dreamers, the diggers of the Earth, those who rammed a piece of steel into the heart of Mother Earth, who cares the length or the latitude.

And there near Hillview came the gush of life, legend, land riches scooped with reason all about him in a hurry of sales and scales, his riches piling up, Alice Hudson suddenly a queen even in her own sadness as the pair joined their own forces. They found an empire to their liking, nothing could stop them, until a spirit from the past from an old trail burial decided to join them.

She woke with a start, and alarm. "Did you just see what I just saw, Tim on horseback rushing to catch up to us. Did you see it, Turf? Oh, my gawd, it's so real!"

Turf was employed in his own dream when she woke him. "I was having my own dream. That section on the northwest side is a sure good addition to grab. I've been warned to start today to wrap it in the coffers. It should be ours."

"Can't you think of anything else, Turf? We've had a warning. We have to pay attention to it. Tim was a stern believer in dreams and warnings put in your lap. He always said so. I remember when he first spoke about those Indians. It was the night before the attack. He knew it was coming."

"That's you just hearing his words, like an echo, coming from back there where we buried him. And no cowboy's horse ever wants a ghost perched on his saddle. They'd go crazy. Toss him off in a second, on the first four-legged leap off the ground. Rest easy, queen of the May. It's not a problem for us."

He stretched his hand to touch her and he could feel her shrinking in the bed, withdrawal controlling her, as though she wanted to depart, disappear, leave this whole word of oil.

"Listen to me," he said. "In the first place, it was Indians who found oil, used it, made it special and then it became big medicine. But they never knew how big it was going to get, how gigantic, and even now I have a hard time trying to measure how big. It'll probably be bigger than me, but I want to try to get as much as I can, and that has to include you."

She swarmed around him. "Then you have to think about what I say, every word I say. We have had a warning. We have to listen."

"Okay," Turf Malloy said, "I'll pay attention to your words. I'll go for a simple ride to the north west to look at that chunk of earth soon to be ours."

When he sensed the horse's motions were becoming exorbitant, he tried to pull him back, was suddenly impelled into the air, came crashing down on a rock, his last sight being the liquid oozing from the side of the rock.

About the Author

Thomas F. Sheehan served in the 31st Infantry, Korea, 1951-52, and graduated Boston College, 1956. Books include *Epic Cures; Brief Cases, Short Spans; The Saugus Book; This Rare Earth & Other Flights; Ah, Devon Unbowed; Reflections from Vinegar Hill.* eBooks include *Korean Echoes (nominated for a Distinguished Military Award)*, *The Westering,* (nominated for National Book Award); from *Danse Macabre* are *Murder at the Forum*, *Death of a Lottery Foe, Death by Punishment, An Accountable Death and Vigilantes East. A Collection of Friends, From the Quickening, In the Garden of Long Shadows*, *The Nations*, *Where Skies Grow Wide*, *Cross Trails*, *The Cowboys, Between Mountain and River, Beside the Broken Trail,* and *Catch a Wagon to the Stars* were published by Pocol Press, and *Six Guns, Inc.,* by *Nazar Look,* in Romania. Sheehan has multiple works at these sites: *Rosebud, Linnet's Wings, Serving House Journal*, *Copperfield Review*, *KYSO Flash, La Joie Magazine, Soundings East, Literary Orphans*, *Indiana Voices Journal, Frontier Tales*, *Western Online Magazine, Provo Canyon Review*, *Nazar Look, Eastlit, Rope & Wire Magazine, Ocean Magazine, The Literary Yard, Green Silk Journal, Fiction on the Web, The Path, Faith-Hope and Fiction, The Cenacle, etc*. Sheehan's tales have produced 30 Pushcart nominations, and five Best of the Net nominations (and one winner) and short story awards from *Nazar Look* for 2012-2015. *Swan River Daisy* was recently released by KY Stories and *Back Home in Saugus*, 200 pages, 90,000 words, and a chapbook, *Small Victories for the Soul,* are on proposal. (His Amazon Author's Page, Tom Sheehan – is on the Amazon site.)

Made in the USA
Middletown, DE
15 August 2019